"Have you a drink of water to spare?"

His low baritone rumbled, very pleasant to the ear, but Polly always had a hard time with heavy Australian accents.

"Water? Certainly." She dug out her water can from beneath the wagon seat and extended it.

He snatched the can from her hand and drank long and deep, like a camel just come home. Presently he took a deep breath and handed it back. " 'Preciate it, mum. How far to Corley Bore?"

"Fifteen miles." She stowed the can under the seat.

His face melted, the expression of a small child promised candy and then denied it. She still feared him; he stood a good six feet tall and square-shouldered. But her heart tugged, too. Fifteen miles was a long hot walk. "Meeting someone in Corley?"

"Looking for work."

"They're probably still hiring up north at Magadura station. I doubt you'd find anything in Corley." She studied his face. Those soft gray eyes snapped unusually bright and his cheeks looked flushed, not all sun color. "Are you all right?"

"Right enough. You an American?"

"Until I married an Aussie five years ago. I'm Polly Chase—Mrs. Peter Chase." She hesitated only briefly. "I can take you part way to Magadura, then you'd have only eight miles left to walk."

"Thank you, mum. 'Preciate it." He ambled to the tailgate, pulled himself up favoring his right arm, then crawled into the wagon bed between the sugar and the tea. When she glanced around again, the man appeared to have fallen asleep, his head vibrating against a heavy sack. Something was definitely wrong.

Now what was she going to do with Peter away at the war and this burly stranger on her hands—either sick or drunk or some fugitive from justice. *Peter, oh Peter, where are you? Please come home!*

OPAL FIRE

Sandy Dengler

BOOKS

of the Zondervan Publishing House
Grand Rapids, Michigan

A Note From The Author:
I love to hear from my readers! You may correspond with me by writing:

        Sandy Dengler
        1415 Lake Drive, S.E.
        Grand Rapids, MI 49506

OPAL FIRE
Copyright © 1986 by The Zondervan Corporation
Grand Rapids, Michigan

Serenade/Saga is an imprint of Zondervan Publishing House,
1415 Lake Drive, S.E., Grand Rapids, Michigan 49506.

ISBN 0-310-47412-4

Edited by Anne Severance
Designed by Kim Koning

Printed in the United States of America

86 87 88 89 90 91 / 10 9 8 7 6 5 4 3 2 1

*For our friends who
speak to God
in Strine*

CHAPTER 1

SHE FIRST SAW HIM coming when he was still three miles off, because that's the way Australia is. The road narrowed to a single point beyond the ears of her gentle wagon horse. It narrowed to another point behind the wagon's tailgate. The horizon sketched a ruler-straight line, eye level, all the way around her. The last heat of late summer made the level line shimmer and dance.

Paulette Belinda Upshaw Chase didn't really mind the April heat, particularly since autumn was hard upon her. Autumn would cool things off. She didn't mind the ironing-board expanse of vastness, or the fact that the land on the horizon looked exactly like that beside her wagon here. She had trudged up enough vertical hills in her youth in San Francisco; flatness means easy going. Besides, she liked distance and far-ness.

A woman out here in the middle of nowhere was vulnerable, though. She felt that vulnerability now as the distance closed steadily between her and that stranger. What Polly really needed was one of those dandy motor cars. Wealthy people were driving them commonly, so they must not be some passing fad. In fact, the latest newsweekly, dated April 6, 1919, showed Prime Minister William Hughes himself sitting in a big open motor car. It was not that Polly harbored pretentions of wealth and status. Perish the thought! She was a farmer's wife—a cocky's wife, if you preferred the local vernacular. It was simply that a motor car was the perfect thing out in this vastness.

You could go farther and faster than a horse and wagon travels, and motor cars were safety factors for lone lasses like herself. Should some saucy larrikin accost her, a mere flick of the steering wheel would crush his nasty intentions. Polly smirked. Alas, for her destiny was not to drive a shiny motor car but an unkempt roan mare. Jewel, dear sluggish aging Jewel, was a farm horse without pretention to wealth or status.

That sundowner was now a quarter mile away and approaching her slowly along the road.

Perhaps Polly's potential problem was not the lack of a motor car but rather the fact that she was in her prime, slight of build, dark-haired, dark-eyed and what men called pretty. Good looks definitely made one more conspicuous and more subject to leers and suggestions. If she were old and dowdy she would feel far less uneasy around strangers. But then, who wants to be old and dowdy? Polly reflected for a moment on the difficult choices confronting women, dilemmas with no right answers, and decided that that was her whole life in a pea-pod—all questions to decide and no right answers. The jackaroo was a hundred feet ahead and still coming. She pulled her buggy whip from its stock and laid it on the seat beside her.

The stranger walked slowly, shuffling along the roadside. Was he a sheepman or drover? He wore that kind of hat, all stained and saggy from long years in the weather. He carried no swag of any kind. A faded brown coat drooped over his shoulders. Its tails flapped loose around his thighs. Why should he wear his coat in this heat? His blue shirt, nearly as filthy as his boots, gaped open halfway down the front. He carried his saddle not over his shoulder as most men do, but hanging off his left hip. One stirrup was tied up but the other had fallen loose. It thumped against his shin with each step and he seemed not to notice. Several days growth of beard and a rich, deep suntan darkened his face almost to the sandy-brown of his hair. The face was nice, evensay handsome, but that hardly guaranteed that the fellow was not dangerous. Polly could see no gun or knife, but that was no guarantee, either.

He stopped in the roadway and just stood there watching her, almost expectantly. With some misgiving, Polly drew Jewel to a halt, not too close. The little roan shook her head.

"Have you a drink of water to spare?" His low baritone rumbled, very pleasant to the ear, but Polly always had a hard time with heavy Australian accents. His was one of the heaviest she had heard.

"Water. Certainly." She dug out her water can from beneath the wagon seat and extended it.

His saddle dropped in the dirt. He snatched the can out of her hand and drank long and heavily like a camel just come home. He must be one of those totally left-handed people. His right hand remained at his side.

Presently he took a deep breath and handed her can back. He seemed almost embarrassed to have nearly emptied it. " 'Preciate it, mum. How far to Corley Bore?"

"Fifteen miles." She stowed her can back under the seat.

His face melted, the expression of a small child promised candy and then denied it. She still feared him; he stood a good six feet tall and square-shouldered. But her heart tugged, too. Fifteen miles is a long hot road to lug a saddle down.

"Are you meeting someone in Corley?"

"Looking for work."

"They're probably still hiring up north at Magadura station. I doubt there's anything in Corley." She studied his face. Those soft gray eyes snapped unusually

9

bright and his cheeks looked flushed. That wasn't all
sun color. "Are you all right?"

"Right enough. American?"

"Until I married an Aussie five years ago. I still can't
accept the fact that I'm the one with the accent." She
hesitated only a little. "I can take you part way to
Magadura. You'd have only eight miles left to walk."

He stood a long moment, looking back dejectedly
the way he had just come. "I suppose—" His eyes
drifted up to hers. "Thank you, mum. 'Preciate it."
He picked up his saddle and ambled to the tailgate. It
seemed to take special effort to heave his saddle up
into the wagon bed. Slowly, like an aged pensioner, he
crawled in behind it.

"What's your name?"

"Comb Stole, mum."

She frowned. "Spell it, please."

"C-O-L-M S-T-A-W-E-L-L, Comb Stole." He
sat heavily and rubbed his face with his left hand. The
right lay useless in his lap.

"Polly Chase. Mrs. Peter Chase. Welcome aboard."
She shook Jewel's lines. Eager to see her manger again,
the mare lurched forward.

*Well, Polly, you dumb banana, now what? You moon
one minute about wanting a motor car for protection
and then you invite a total stranger into your wagon.
Obviously this is but one more in the long line of your
famous lousy decisions.*

She hated herself when she thought out a fine game
of life in her dreams and then let her actions ruin it.
And it happened constantly. What if he didn't want to
leave her wagon once she reached the Y? What if he
decided to come home with her instead of walking another eight miles north? She must be very careful not
to let slip that she lived alone, that Peter was away.
Let this burly stranger think a three-hundred-pound
ex-wrestler was awaiting her safe return.

She listened for any movement, threatening or otherwise. She heard none. Presently she glanced behind.

Stretched out between the sugar and the tea, the man appeared to have fallen asleep. His head vibrated on the wagon bed and even clunked occasionally. Something was definitely wrong.

Curiosity finally overcame caution. She wrapped Jewel's lines around the brake and clambered into the back. She knelt between the flour and the tea and carefully laid a hand on his forehead. He opened his eyes, glanced at her and closed them again.

"Do you know what's wrong with you?"

"Sorry?"

"You claimed you were right enough. You lied. Your head is hot enough to fry emu eggs."

"It'll pass," he mumbled.

"If it's contagious, I'm an even bigger fool than I thought I was a minute ago." Disgusted with her own soft-headedness, she slopped some water on her handkerchief, dropped it on his face for him to adjust as he wished, and climbed back onto the seat.

Well, that explained why he wore his coat. When you're fevered you feel chilled even as your body temperature is climbing. And if he still felt cold, his fever, already high, was getting higher. Polly knew diddly about the treatment of fevers. What to do? Another vexing decision to make. Eliza! Surely Eliza Belfour up at Magadura, mistress of one of the area's largest stations, would know all about fevers; she was raising five children.

But then, Maggie was good, too. Maggie Minnanong, half white and half Aborigine, lived alone. But Polly knew she had raised several children (and had gone through at least three husbands so far). Maggie lived only six miles from here, while Magadura was still a good eighteen miles off. Choosing the closest port in a storm, Polly hauled Jewel aside and started off cross country. She would leave this Stawell fellow with Maggie and solve all her problems at once.

Weary old Jewel was nearly all tucked up by the time she plodded into Maggie's farmyard. The sun hung

11

yellow near the shimmering horizon. Maggie's old horse Binta flung its ragged head over the paddock fence and whinnied eagerly. He'd never done that before. Maggie's milk cow even greeted her with a low, throaty moo.

Frowning, Polly stood up. "Maggie? Maggie, you here?"

Binta nickered impatiently. The animals' agitation bothered Polly. They usually paid no notice when she dropped by.

"*Maaaa-geeee*!" Polly listened. A seed of uneasiness planted itself beneath her breastbone and began to grow. Maggie often went out for the day, but she never neglected her animals. Maggie was a creature of ritual. She should be here.

When Maggie's shaky little house burned down three years ago, she had snorted a cheerful "Good riddance!" and built herself a humpy, the traditional Aborigine brush shelter. Polly hopped down and crossed to it. It smelled funny inside, but then it usually did. It was getting too dark to see well. "Maggie?"

Binta and the cow sang a duet. Polly walked across the yard to them. Every wisp of hay was gone and their water trough was empty. The seed of uneasiness blossomed into fear.

"Pump 'em some water. I'll go look around." Colm Stawell's voice made her jump. He stood right behind her and she hadn't heard him. "Maggie wear shoes?"

"No, but she usually wears a dress. About this tall." Polly held a hand near her nose. "Halfway in color between black and white. Light brown."

He nodded and ambled off toward the humpy. She primed the pump from the can in the shed and started to work. The eager animals drank it as fast as she could pump it. It took her some minutes to realize that somehow Mr. Stawell had taken over the situation. He had issued orders and she had obeyed without a second thought. Who did he think he was, anyway?

She managed to fill the trough eventually, then forked

12

the manger to overflowing with hay. He came back across the yard still at that easy stroll. Didn't he ever move fast? They met in the middle, near Jewel's head. He looked grim. "Maggie own a gun?"

"A sixteen-gauge shotgun with a taped stock. She rarely uses it. Usually she just bops a goanna on the head with her waddy. Her stick."

"A dog?"

"Six months ago. He got killed last spring—October or November."

"Any friends who wear boots?"

"No. What did you find out there?"

"Boot prints and patches of dry blood. Dog tracks; dingos or bushrangers' mutts."

"Bushrangers!" Polly shook her head. "We've never had a problem around here with unsavory sorts. Blood? Maybe she cut up a kangaroo. She does that. Or—" She knew even as she spoke that she was grasping at straws. When Maggie killed a 'roo or anteater, she dressed and bled the game where she killed it rather than carry it at its heaviest. And it was highly unlikely she'd take game this close to the buildings. And the neglected animals—she glanced back at Binta and the cow.

Polly looked at the darkening sky. No clouds. As soon as the rain started the pastures would green up and these animals would not need hay. But that was *someday*. Should she leave them here and return in a few days, or take them and risk giving Maggie the scare that her animals had been stolen? Should they stay the night here, or go on? Decisions, decisions.

She could make one decision. Jewel knew the way home even in darkness, and the moon was coming into its first quarter. Polly would go home. And what about this stranger? Mr. Stawell draped his arm over Jewel's back and sagged against the mare. He looked ready to fall over. Perhaps he could simply stop here until his strength returned. There was water in easy access, and probably some food. He'd have milk if the cow had not dried up. Maggie wouldn't mind.

Maggie. Stubborn, independent, bush-wise Maggie. Maggie was tougher by far than this wild land. What could have happened to her? Why bootprints? She didn't even know anyone who wore boots—not since her husband died. If foul play had overtaken Maggie, Polly was doomed, for Polly was nowhere near as strong and capable as was her dark, stocky little friend.

Polly motioned toward her wagon. "My place is three hours from here. You can ride along if you wish. Travel up to Magadura from there."

Now why oh why had she just said that, because he had taken her at her word and was already stumbling toward the tailgate? *Polly, you silly galah, you want that fellow to remain here and you invite him home. How could you. . . .* She remembered her water can was nearly empty and took the few extra minutes to refill it and top off the animals' trough. When she climbed up onto the seat with her heavy water can, Mr. Stawell appeared already to have fallen into a fitful sleep.

With a heavy sigh she released the brake and clucked to Jewel. Whether or not she knew anything about fevers, this stranger needed her help. Quite possibly Maggie lay out in the bush, perhaps even close by, needing help. Or possibly Maggie and this stranger would both do perfectly well on their own. Then again maybe both were dying, beyond reach of anyone's help. Was Mr. Stawell's fever the symptom of some dreaded and dangerous disease?

For the millionth time Polly yearned for Peter. She needed Peter. She wanted Peter. She had done without her husband now for nearly five years. She could handle the day-to-day decisions and keep things going. But when something like this descended upon her. . . .

Peter, oh Peter, where are you? Please come home!

CHAPTER 2

"IT'S A LONESOME WASH without a man's shirt in it."
So the saying went.

True, true, true. Polly smiled a mite bitterly to herself as she felt this blue chambray shirt on her clothesline. She squeezed under the heavy seams. It seemed dry enough to iron. She unpinned it and took it inside. His other clothes she had washed yesterday. The shirt here had needed an extra day's soaking.

She wandered into the kitchen in no particular hurry. She touched a wetted finger to the bottom of an iron. Hot enough. It had better be. The cookstove was making an oven out of the whole kitchen. She filled her narrow-waisted Coke bottle, jammed the cork-and-tin sprinkler head into it, and sprinkled the shirttails. She ironed his shirt with more care than she usually paid her own clothes, and she could not say why.

She left both flatirons on the stovetop and sat down beside her sewing desk in the sitting room. It took her perhaps twenty minutes to properly mend the long rip in his shirt sleeve. It appeared to have been made with a sharp object, probably a knife. All that soaking notwithstanding, the bloodstains were still there. They

15

had not really come out, but at least they were now muted down to more conservative colors, evensay tasteful shades of brown. Was this rip in his shirt, and the matching rip in his arm, the result of some clumsy accident? A fight? She had asked him, and he seemed then too muddled to give her a forthright answer.

She held her work up and admired it privately. Polly Chase might be deficient in many skills, but how she could make a needle fly! This repair job was neat in every stitch, and firm. It wouldn't rip out again soon. She made her pillow lace the same way. And her embroidery was as near perfect as she could manage. She preferred things that way.

She glanced up on the shelf at her lace-making bolster. She should either get it down and use it, or dust it. There was the velvet-covered drum, free-turning, surrounded by the broad, sloping velvet skirt. On it Polly could tie intricate laces six inches wide or a bit more, with uncountable bobbins lying all around the velvet skirts in orderly pairs—and never a mistake. That took a certain degree of skill.

Farming skills? Deficient. In fact she was down to two chickens, both old enough to qualify for pensions, and a cow that surrendered milk grudgingly, if at all. Only the rabbits did well. They multiplied like—like rabbits. That reminded her; had she fed Muffin today? She must check on the way out.

With the flatirons she touched up the mended shirt, then quietly hung it on the straightback chair in the bedroom. She leaned a minute in the bedroom doorway to watch Mr. Stawell. He was sleeping peacefully, restfully, his breathing measured and even. His general color in his face seemed somehow better today.

Two days ago Polly had known nothing about fevers. Today she might still be ignorant about disease, but she could tell you a thing or two about fever from infection. It's a poor day you don't learn something.

She upended the flatirons on trivets to cool and put the ironing board away. Her house was in order. Now—

for the outside. She stuffed her thick hair bun up into her straw gardening hat, for the sun was still fierce in April.

Muffin had indeed been fed. The furry brown bunny sat contently, up to her ears in rutabaga greens and old lettuce, munching rapid-fire with that busy little mouth. Polly fetched a scoop of chicken scratch from the barn, her next chore.

In a flurry of black and white, a pied butcherbird settled to the ground ten feet from Polly's shoe. He cocked his head and watched, waiting for some tasty morsel to fall his way. Polly shooed him and threw the last of her scratch to the hens on her way to check the water trough. It doesn't take long to feed two chickens.

She swirled her finger in Jewel's water and thought about Binta. It had been nearly three days since they had stopped at Maggie's place. She ought to go back, but frankly, she was afraid to. What if Maggie had indeed met with foul play, and the foul players still lurked about?

Polly spent fifteen minutes in the garden, though there weren't fifteen minutes' worth of chores here. She pulled a few weeds and checked next year's cabbage seedlings. Here were two more squash ready. More squash. Sigh. She broke them off the vine and tucked one under each arm. The garden was dying for the year. The beans and peas were done, the potatoes dug, the early carrots long gone. Next spring's carrots, a few inches high, were nowhere near ready. If Peter walked into the yard this minute, he would be proud of the way she had learned to plant throughout the year. When he left, she and he both knew next to nothing about gardening.

She snorted at the bitter twist of humor, if you could call it that. She had lived here in lonely isolation for almost five years, doing nothing more than wait for Peter to return from the war. Were Peter to show up now, after all that time she was alone, he would find a strange man in his bed. And the way fate loved to

17

pull little pranks on Polly, this would be the very thing to bring the prodigal husband home. No matter; dear, gentle Peter was an understanding soul who constantly believed the best in everybody. She paused, smiling as the memory of Peter washed warm over her.

Polly hoped the stranger would soon be well enough to travel on up to Magadura. She did not particularly like sleeping on the lumpy little davenport in the parlor, but he needed the only bed more than she did. Until yesterday evening he had been too weak and feverish to do much more than sit up long enough to sip a bit of soup.

She smiled to herself as she let herself out the garden gate. There is a certain satisfaction in helping a man who cannot help himself. And for the first time in years she was paying attention to meals. Within a year of Peter's leaving, she had fallen into the habit of cooking up whatever happened to be ripe in the garden. She would eat almost nothing but peas for weeks, then nothing but string beans or broad beans. She knew it wasn't the best of dietary practice, but it was certainly easier. With Mr. Stawell around she was at least preparing meat-and-vegetable soups. He seemed to appreciate them so.

His gratitude made her service more satisfying. He rarely said much, and what few words he spoke were always polite and well-seasoned and usually included "thank you" or "appreciate it." He obviously meant it, too. She took her time strolling up the path. She came around the corner of the house and stopped with a gasp.

He looked so much like Peter standing there at the washbasin, leaning toward the broken bit of mirror, his face half foamy with lather. He turned and nodded. "G'day, mum. Thought I'd scrape this fur off before I forgot what my face looks like."

She grinned. "You're sure you're strong enough to lift the razor? I wouldn't want you cutting your throat."

He smiled, too. "I'll use two hands, right-o?"

18

"Porridge all right for breakfast?"

"Fine, mum, thank you." He returned to that mysterious male ritual of shaving.

Polly went inside and laid her squash on the drainboard. She had watched Peter shave often. Just as Peter did, Mr. Stawell now would be contorting his face, trying to stretch round skin flat, trying to make the little corners by his nose somehow larger and easier to scrape. In many ways all men were pretty much alike. She pushed the porridge pot closer to the middle of the stovetop and brought two deep dishes off the shelf. She thought of Peter—but the image of Mr. Stawell intruded. Why should that be?

He came in presently, just as the porridge began making those clumsy poofing bubbles. He crossed to the kitchen table and sat heavily in the chair by the window—Peter's favorite place. She served the two porringers and paused beside him long enough to lay a hand on his face and neck. "I do believe you're about over it."

He dug into the porridge and didn't mind its heat. Good. The first sign of good health is a good appetite.

She poured coffee for them both and sat down across from him. "Would you do me a favor, Mr. Stawell?"

"Gladly."

"You're a man of too few words. You never mentioned that gash in your arm, yet it was so dirty and infected it took me an hour to clean it out. It must have hurt terribly, and I'm sure the infection was the source of your fever. I'm amazed you didn't die of blood poisoning. But you never explained how you got it, though I asked. Nor why you should be walking down the middle of the road a mile beyond Woop Woop carrying your saddle. No horse—or anything. Might you please satisfy my curiosity with a few clear and complete sentences?"

He chuckled, a barely audible baritone rumble. "I was more or less headed toward Broken Hill, thinking maybe of becoming a miner, when a couple or three sundowners joined me. They intended they should take over my worldly possessions and I intended they shouldn't. Managed to drive them off, but they got this one good lick in with a knife. Escaped with my horse and swag. So I changed plans and came south, since I didn't feel up to walking clear to Broken Hill." He ran his finger down his sleeve. "Thank you for mending my shirt."

"You're welcome. Sorry I couldn't get the bloodstains out completely. At least now you look like a sloppy coffee drinker and not a war casualty. Are you a drover?"

He nodded. "Worked on a station up near Marree until it went into receivership. What little money came out of it went to the silvertails, not the hired hands."

"Silvertails?"

"Bankers and city blokes." He stared off beyond the window a few minutes, sipping his coffee. "Since my razor's in my swag somewhere in the bush, I borrowed your husband's there. It hasn't been stropped for a while."

"Almost five years. You see, Peter prides himself on being a man of God. Oh, he isn't an ordained minister or anything, but he's—well, very enthusiastic about his faith. When he heard the army needed chaplains, he took the train to Melbourne to talk about helping. They signed him on the spot and off he went."

"Five years ago. Nineteen-fourteen."

"Mid-winter. August seventeen, to be precise. He sent me one letter from Egypt. It glowed. He was so happy to be serving God that way, he said. It was short, but Peter was never a letter-writer. Even during courtship he didn't write anything I could tie a blue ribbon around and store in a trunk. So it's not surprising I don't hear from him much."

"Just one letter? You sure he's still alive?"

"He must be. The army still sends me his monthly paycheck. He arranged that before he left. His pay is enough to meet the mortgage payments and keep me going. Garden produce brings in a little extra, and I make lace. Pillow lace. Time-consuming, but I have lots of time."

"How long married before he left?"

"Four months. April twenty-two." She sat erect and twisted to see the calendar beside the stove. "Our fifth anniversary is six days off. Wouldn't it be wonderful if he came back on our anniversary!"

The corners of Mr. Stawell's mouth kinked up slightly. "Except that my presence might be something of an embarrassment to you. Appearances. How big is this place?"

He had shifted subjects so quickly she had to think a moment. "About one and a half square miles. Just over a thousand acres. Two sheep paddocks, but we don't have sheep yet."

"Enough water?"

"Enough for up at the house here, yes. And a friend says it would be a simple matter to reach water with a bore on the west side, but I haven't done that either. Without cattle or sheep, we really don't need water on the west side."

"Your husband bought the house and barns along with the land."

"Yes. How do you know?"

"I noticed daylight through your bedroom roof in a couple spots. A house less than five years old shouldn't need re-roofing yet. It's a grouse farm, though. In fact, an excellent farm. If your husband knows anything at all about farming, you two will turn this into a very profitable place."

"Curious you should say it that way. He and I don't know a thing about farming. He got a good offer when we were planning to marry. It seemed like a good deal, he said."

"He was right. My saddle in the barn?"

"Just inside the doors to the right."

He nodded and lapsed into thought of some sort. Polly gathered up the dishes and immersed them in the dishpan. She gestured toward him with the coffeepot and he shook his head. She dwelt a moment on the thought of that. Peter made non-stop conversation every waking moment. He verbalized everything. This man trimmed his words as a butcher trims a roast—no waste, no fat, no gristle. Presently he thanked her for breakfast and walked outside.

She should clean out the rabbit cage today, before Muffin gave birth to her next litter. Now was as good a time as any. She dried her hands on her apron as she stepped out into the bright morning sun.

Mr. Stawell had flopped his saddle in the dirt outside the barn. He was doing something to the underside of it. Polly noted that he still avoided using his sore right arm. She crossed to inquire about it. "Is it broken?"

He smiled, ignoring her question, "My private bank. Those drongos got the two quid in my swag, but they missed this." With his pocketknife he was digging under the leather stitching near the back end. He popped something out into his hand, folded the knife and stood up. "I realize now I was sicker than I thought. You went to a lot of work and plain discomfort for me. Even washed and mended my clothes. Just saying thank you doesn't seem like much. Dead-set, you'll be able to use this a lot better than I can." He dropped something small and hard into her hand and closed her fingers over it. "With thanks."

It was a gemstone, a queen's gem, the biggest opal Polly had ever seen. It was polished and trimmed into a smooth oval, the long axis more than an inch in length. Polly had never seen an opal so rich a blue. Its deep pearlescent color caught the sunbeams and flashed them back to her, ray by fiery ray, when she moved it the least bit.

"It's beautiful—" she stammered "but I can't accept this! Peter would be the first to agree that charity begins at home and I was only doing you a favor. I can't. I really can't."

"If I didn't want you and your husband to have it,

I wouldn't have dug it out." His warm hand closed her fingers back over it. The stone turned instantly dark in the shadow. "Thank you, mum." He grabbed his saddle and hitched it up on his hip.

She stood stunned a moment until it sank in that he was leaving. "Wait! You can't go." She ran forward and stepped in front of him. "You're not well enough to walk all the way to Magadura."

His soft gray eyes settled on hers. She spoke quickly. "In a day or two, if you wish, I'll take you up there in the wagon. I'd love to see Eliza again anyway, I really would. It's been months since we got together." Less than an hour ago she was wondering when he would leave. Now she could not bear to see him go. She couldn't understand her own fickleness.

He shook his head. "Your man might return while you were gone. That wouldn't do. I'll get on fine."

"Please don't. I'm afraid that—" Of course! That was it! "I'm afraid to stay here alone now, because of what may have happened to Maggie. And I really should go back over there and check on Binta and the cow. They're probably out of water again if she's gone. I mean, if someone did something to her. I mean—and they're still around." She clamped her teeth over her lower lip.

He nodded slowly. "That's a fair point."

"And you really should take it easy a few days yet. You still look pretty dicky."

The saddle slid down his hip a few inches. He studied her eyes a moment, digesting, thinking. "I'll take it easy out in the barn, though. Give you back your bed. A blanket in the haymow will do me just fine."

She sighed in relief. "Thank you. Understand I can't afford a hired man, and I don't expect you to work for only your keep. It's more than enough that I feel safer with you around. There's probably nothing to worry about, but—" She flopped her hands helplessly.

"I wouldn't feel very happy with myself if I left and something happened. I ought stay around at least until

23

we find out about your Maggie. Or until your man gets back." He turned around and shuffled back toward the barn with his saddle.

Polly drew a deep breath. She opened her hand to admire the opal again. She held it in two fingers and tilted it this way and that. The fire flashed and sparkled. She raised her eyes from the blue dazzle to the barn door. Mr. Stawell was walking inside to put his saddle away, melting into dark shadows. She closed her hand over the stone. The fire went out.

Polly Chase pulled another long breath in through her nose and headed back to the house to finish tidying her kitchen—just in case Peter should return today.

CHAPTER 3

IT MUST BE THE thick autumn haze making sunset
so colorful tonight. Rich gold washed across the grass
tufts and scrub trees outside Polly's kitchen window.
The whole flat land glowed yellow as far as she could
see.

The tears brimmed up over her eyelids again and
made her nose run. She glanced at the pot of stew on
the stove. It was off to the side and the fire was going
out. So let it get cold. He wouldn't be back to eat it.

She wiped her nose on her sleeve because her hands
were too wet to dig out a hankie. How could she have
been so utterly stupid? She had known this man less
than four days—a drifter, a sundowner, a no-hoper
with no visible means of support. This morning she
had glibly helped him put his saddle on her horse, her
Jewel, and then waved goodbye as he rode away.

She waved goodbye, all right—to Jewel. What would
she tell Peter? That she had encouraged some sweet-
talking man to ride away on his horse? She left the
dishpan, dried her hands on a towel and went back to
the bedroom for another hankie.

She paused at the chest of drawers. The opal lay

beside the oil lamp on the crocheted doily. That opal. She felt like flinging it out the window. He probably stole it somewhere, perhaps from some trusting and unsuspecting woman like herself. It meant nothing to him. But a horse meant a great deal to them both. Polly certainly could not get to town on a gemstone any more than he could ride tc Broken Hill on it. She could not plow the garden come spring, or haul the hayrick in, or pull stumps. If nothing else, this costly, ignorant decision showed how desperately she needed Peter's stable, solid advice, his clear head.

Fatalistically, she tried to convince herself it didn't really matter. What's done was done and no use crying about it. It didn't work. She collapsed on the bed for another sobbing session. Eventually, her passion spent, she dug out a clean hankie and wandered into the parlor.

This sitting room was her escape. Two solid walls of bookshelves held Peter's extensive library and hers. The memory of him sitting in the overstuffed leather chair there by the lamp table almost started her crying again. Then she took her lace-making bolster down off the shelf and lighted her own lamp. She sat and gave the padded cylinder a spin. She hadn't made lace for a week. How many wound bobbins were left? She checked in her little sewing desk here. About thirty. She'd use these and wind more later.

She set the bolster and frame on her sewing desk and chose the pattern with the circles of leaf-stitch. That particular pattern of lace always sold well. She pinned the paper pattern carefully around the bolster and tried in vain to keep her mind on what she was doing. Her memories kept drifting back to the picture of Colm Stawell riding into the morning sun. With her blessing! She might hold a degree in English literature, but her practical judgment wasn't worth a brass razoo.

Viciously she jabbed the pins into the pattern and bolster to begin. She gathered up two bobbins in each hand and paused. Now she really did have to apply herself. Did she start with twists or passeés? She could not remember and she'd woven this pattern a hundred times. *Twist 2nd and 3rd 2X, cross, pin at 1, passeé* . . . that was it. Her hands flicked rapidly. They fell into the familiar rhythm of crossing the bobbins, twisting threads, jamming pins precisely onto the little dots of her worn paper pattern. A broad, lacy strand of edging began to form itself. The work and the sameness of it made her feel better.

She stiffened and sat bolt upright. Did she hear horses' hooves? She hurried to the window. The sun was down now, the twilight nearly too far spent for her to see anything at all. But she was certain that was Colm Stawell returning on Jewel! She ran out into the barnyard.

Jewel was not accustomed to carrying a heavy man. The little roan dragged her feet as she plodded across the dusty yard. Binta slogged along behind Jewel, equally jaded. And here was Maggie's cow on another lead-line.

Mr. Stawell looked even worse tucked up than the sorry horses. He slid off Jewel's back and just stood there, leaning against her. He dipped his head toward Polly. "G'day, mum."

Polly reached out to scratch the cow behind her horns. She bit her lower lip and tried not to think about what this meant.

Mr. Stawell lurched erect. "I tried milking her, but she's dried up."

"About time she brought off another calf anyway. Was their water gone?"

He nodded grimly.

"Did you find any—see any—were there any signs of—"

"Wind erased most of it. I spent maybe four hours walking around there. She hasn't been back since we were there. No Maggie."

She liked Maggie so much, and now the lady was

vanished with a simple, terse "no Maggie." Polly's sigh turned to a sob. She clamped her hand over her mouth.

Two long arms pulled her in against a bulky chest. A broad hand pressed the side of her head against the brown wool coat. She cried again, partly for Maggie and partly in shame. How could she have doubted this man's intentions? Of course he was late getting back. He was still much too weak to cover such distances. He must have had to stop and rest often. Surely he must have felt like just quitting. Yet he put Maggie's animals before his own welfare and here he was. *Shame, shame, shame, Polly!*

The tears subsided. Only then did she realize how comforting his strong arms were. She lifted her head, stepped back and fumbled for her hankie.

He released her instantly and turned to pick at his saddle girth. "I don't want to plant any false hopes, but I didn't find a body, either. If bushrangers killed her they wouldn't have dragged the body very far. I would've found it."

"But she wandered long distances from her house during the day. What if they came on her in the bush?"

"Boot prints all round her humpy. Appears they struggled there, at home. And I called around some. If she was within cooee, she would've heard me."

She tried to see his eyes in the gathering gloom. "If she should come back, do you suppose she'll know what happened to her animals?"

"If she recognizes your horse's bridle, she will. I left it inside her humpy and used hers to ride back."

Polly smiled. "That was clever. And very thoughtful. I guess that's all we can do. Any idea who belongs to the boot prints?"

He shook his head. "So we still don't know if they're gone or if they might show up here. Guess I better stay around awhile, in case."

She nodded. Maggie. She shuddered and squared her shoulders. "Supper's waiting and the manger's filled."

"Thank you, mum. Be right in."

Polly hurried to the kitchen and dragged the stewpot into the middle of the stove. She stuffed some kindling in the box, since the coals were too far gone to touch off large sticks. She grabbed leftover biscuits and laid them directly on the iron plate near the stovepipe. The butter—now where did she put the butter? She touched the side of the coffeepot. It was still hot, so the stew must be. She heard water sloshing in the basin outside.

The sitting room was as cozy as the kitchen, and he looked so tired. She hustled out to the parlor and set the little side table up beside the big leather chair. He'd rest much more comfortably here than in the straight-backed kitchen chairs. She stopped halfway back to the kitchen. Ridiculous! Why was she scurrying around like a chicken with its head cut off? Why was she so flustered and in the mood to serve? Gratitude. That must be it. Gratitude, and a bit of guilt for suspecting the man for being less than noble.

He came in the door, and even though he slouched, practically stumbling, he filled the kitchen.

She motioned toward the sitting room. "I've set you a place at the big leather chair. Rest your weary bones."

"Weary bones, aye. Don't fix me much, please." He left the kitchen, shrugging his coat off as he went.

Peter did that—removed his coat that way. Polly had forgotten the gesture until just now.

She ladled stew, poured coffee and buttered two biscuits. When she carried the meal to the sitting room, she expected to see him sprawled in the chair. Instead, he was squatted down beside the bookshelf, his head cocked to the side, the better to read book spines. He pulled a book and studied its pages a moment. He replaced it and pulled another.

He glanced at his dinner and stood erect stiffly. "Your husband has a fine library here. Wonder if I might read some of his books." He plopped into the leather chair and pulled the side table around over his knees.

"Of course, if you wish." She left the tray on the

side table for him to arrange as he wished and returned to her lace-making bolster. She picked up her bobbins, hesitated a moment reviewing what she'd done, and took it up.

"Your stew tastes extra grouse tonight." He paused to work on a mouthful. She reminded herself that *grouse* was highly complimentary. He swallowed. "During muster last fall, I worked with a larrikin named Homer. Religious chap, but no sobersides. Always happy. He showed me how every man, myself included, needs God's salvation, and how that salvation comes only through Jesus Christ. We had some fair dinkum yabbers on the subject. . . ."

"By which you mean sprightly conversation."

"Yuh." He snickered. "I asked God to give me that salvation and pledged to live in His Son. Then the station went under and we drifted our separate ways. I haven't done anything about my commitment. Don't know a skerrick more about God and Jesus now than I did ten months ago. Your husband's library here is a gold mine for me."

"You and Peter are going to have so much to talk about! He can get on about God and salvation for hours on end."

He finished off a biscuit. "How about you, mum? You ever specifically claim God's salvation?"

"Uh, er, not in so many words. I, uh, never really thought about it." Why did she suddenly feel uncomfortable? She had gone to church as a child; surely that made her a Christian—right? "My parents sent me to a church on Market Street in San Francisco. I grew up in San Francisco."

"There for the quake?"

"Wouldn't have missed it for the world." She smiled. "I should have been terrified, but I was only twelve. It was more an adventure than an ordeal, once the worst of the shaking stopped. Not for my parents, though. The firemen dynamited several long blocks of houses ahead of the fire, trying to cut it off and starve

30

it. It worked. They saved part of the city doing that. But ours was one of the houses they razed." Her fingers paused. "I'll never forget the look on my father's face as Petersons' house exploded, and then MacArthurs'—and then ours." The fingers began to fly again. "We were insured, though. My parents have a lovely home now on the same street. And they didn't lose any children—there are five of us—so they count themselves fortunate. They've said that many a time." She stuck another pin in her work. "I wish more of their optimism had rubbed off on me. Mother writes frequently and her letters are always so cheerful."

He mopped stew broth with the last of his biscuits. "Not many farms in San Francisco."

"Or open space, either. This was all so new to me. Still is, in many ways."

"Regret coming?"

"No. Not at all. But this particular place is quite a way out. I'd like to sell and move in closer to town. Melbourne would be nice, but any town would do. I've had several offers of sale, too, mostly Anzacs coming back from the war and wanting to take up farming. But I can't. The place is in Peter's name. Until he gets back. . . ." Her voice died away.

He moved the little table aside and stood up slowly, awkwardly, an active man in a pensioner's body. He stretched mightily and rubbed his sore arm. "By your leave, I'll go out to bed. Dinner was very good. Thank you."

"Bet you don't stay awake long enough to hear the hay rustle."

He chuckled. "Be sure to lock the door after me when I leave. And you might let your window open a crack, so I can hear your cooee better."

She stood up. "I shall. Thank you for all you did today—for checking at Maggie's, bringing her stock over—everything."

"More'n welcome." He dipped his head in that casual way of his again and walked out through the kitchen.

She followed. He paused at the back door. His gray eyes studied hers for the longest moment. He was thinking something; what was he thinking? She could read nothing in his face.

He was gone. She shot the bolt and leaned against the door awhile. She felt drained suddenly, wearied with the day. She didn't feel like making lace, but it was too early to go to bed. She strolled back to the sitting room, past her sewing desk to the bookshelves.

Which two books had caught his eye? She knelt where he had knelt and called on her memory. This one and this one. She pulled them both. *Foxe's Book of Martyrs*, and *Young's Analytical Concordance*, revised. Did Colm Stawell own a Bible? If he did it was in his swag, lost. Peter had taken his favorite King James, all dog-eared and worn, and left his like-new edition here. Polly pulled it from the upper-left corner shelf. And next to it was Peter's American Standard, 1901, his gift from Polly. She pulled that, too, and laid both Bibles on the side table by the leather chair.

She gathered up the dishes and carried them to the kitchen. She would wash them in the morning. Perhaps she was tired enough to go to bed now, after all. She stopped on her way to the bedroom and looked at the leather chair with the Bibles waiting beside it.

She smiled and nodded.

Peter would approve.

CHAPTER 4

PERHAPS IT WAS THE dusty haze that tended to lift off the land in late afternoon which made sunset so vivid. Even pre-sunset and post-sunset, if such could be called so, were vivid. The sun swam low now, in its light gold phase. Before long it would don its orange phase, then its red phase, then leave behind a wash of purple as it slid west toward Maine.

Polly didn't really have to drive Jewel. Here was one splendid advantage of a horse over a motor car. Jewel knew where the feedbox was, and Polly need do nothing at all to get there. She finished her article in *The Bulletin* as the reins lay slack in her hands.

They were coming up on the farm now, at last. The south paddock, fenced in split-rail along the road here, stretched out to the left toward the weary sun. Jewel left the road without being told and followed the coarse dirt lane toward home.

Polly put the magazine aside, frowning. The farm looked different tonight. There went the fence snaking along the side of the lane. And there in the distance were the gray buildings that a less sympathetic eye might call ramshackle.

That just goes to show how much the unsympathetic eye knows, she thought. True, the barn wanted a little work here and there. True, the sheepfold might be rebuilt, were Polly to install any sheep. The water trough was mended in half a dozen places by pitch and in one place by a broken kitchen knife jammed in along with a rag.

And the house could stand some improvements eventually, too. The ceilings in the kitchen and sitting room were the only ceilings. The bedroom and pantry had no ceilings. Beyond the rafters, up in the dark and silent eaves, only the roof planking itself and the wooden shingles protected Polly from the seasonal rains.

But then, if she installed a ceiling in the bedroom, she ought to put a ventilator window in the eaves, and as soon as she did that, they'd be invaded by swallows and mice and bandicoots and heaven-knows-what-else. She might as well leave well enough alone.

Jewel's pace was picking up a little. The windmill turned casually, at the mercy of a listless breeze. The chickens—both of them—were apparently at roost now. This was Polly's favorite time of day on the farm. It was a silent time, a thoughtful time, a time neither dark nor yet still light, where the mind can pause from the hectic work of day before slipping on to the sleep of night.

The little flock of galahs which hung about the water trough and the coolibah trees gurgled and crabbed at each other. Vivid pink cockatoos with bushy white hats? They would be prizes in any aviary back in America, yet here they flew wild in immense flocks at times. And the little green budgerigars, the frosty white cockatoos—in five years, Polly had never been able to enure herself to the dazzle and wonder of these glorious, exotic birds.

Here was that place where Jewel had leaned too hard on the top rail. The broken rail, in two pieces for nearly a year, was gone. In its place a bright yellow rail, brand-new, promised firm support for horses who knew where the grass was always greener.

Up ahead, new lumber in the barn door painted a brilliant streak of yellow down the dingy gray wood. For years, that door had sagged so badly Polly could neither open nor close it completely. It was closed now and fastened with a yellow wooden peg, so Colm must have fixed the sag when he replaced the broken weatherboarding.

The windmill didn't talk to her. It must have been greased. Polly was not fond of heights, or she would have greased it long ago.

But where was Colm? Without a hint from Polly, Jewel jogged over to the rejuvenated barn door and stood patiently, waiting to be divested of her harness. Polly climbed stiffly down and scooped up a sugar sack. She might as well take an armload with her to the house.

From somewhere in the sky a hammer pounded. So much for that deliciously silent moment hammocked between day and night. She left the sugar on the porch and walked around the house to investigate.

Colm stood atilt on the steep roof above the bedroom. He was walking about up there in stockings, a hammer in his hand, his boots and coat in a pile by the cabbage tree and his sleeves rolled up above his elbows. New yellow shakes like freckles spattered all over the weathered roof.

"G'day, mum!" he called. He pointed to a white strip of paper sticking out of the roof. "That's the last one. Go inside and make sure I got them all." He picked up a yellow shake and cautiously inched his way to the paper flag.

She pulled her hat off as she stepped into the cool darkness. He hadn't built a fire today at all; the house felt a little dank. His pounding gave her the sensation that she had stepped inside a bass drum. She walked back and forth in the bedroom searching for all the familiar little slivers of light in the roof.

She called loudly, "I can't see any daylight!"

She heard something from up on the roof about "everything being apples," then some scuffling sounds. Well, she smiled to herself, everything was not quite apples: Peter wasn't back yet, but the farm was in far better shape now than it had been just a month ago. Mr. Stawell was a worker, paid or not.

He might not have started a fire, but he had the wood laid in the stove. She touched a match to it and slammed the firebox door. By the time she brought the sugar inside and found her apron, Colm was carrying in the first load of groceries.

"Trip go all right, mum?"

"Found everything on the list except brass screws. No one has that size brass screws, so I got steel."

"Good enough. Find a right pair of nippers?"

"I hope so. They were two quid and five, but the hardware clerk assured me they're just what you want for shoeing. With the farrier charging a quid and six just to trim Jewel's feet, that seemed a good investment. Oh, and Peter's check arrived on schedule. But the mail came so late that I already had my banking and buying finished, and I wanted to leave town early this morning before the bank opened, so I just brought it home. I'll bank it next month." She laid her mail on the table beside him.

He frowned at it. "May I?" What was he looking at? He studied the paycheck envelope a moment and picked it up. "Drawn on Melbourne."

"Has been for years. Why?"

"Army usually pays overseas checks out of Sydney or Perth." He looked at her. "You certain Peter's still overseas?"

"I have no idea where he is. But if he's home in Australia here, surely he'd come or at least drop me a note. I mean, I could visit him or whatever. Wouldn't a national army pay its soldiers from the nation's capital?"

"Probably." But he didn't seem to change his mind

at all. His lips pushed in and out. "Ever write to the army and ask where he is? Put a tracer on him?"

"Can you do that?"

He smiled. "Yes, you can. I'll help you if you want to."

"Yes! I'd appreciate it very much. Ah. But now—while the tea water is heating up and the kidney pie is warming, let's unload the wagon. I suppose you noticed my purchase."

He followed her outside. "Where'd you buy them?"

"This lady on the edge of town had a hand-drawn sign up: 'Chooks.' Since I only have two left, and they produce three eggs a week at most—" She hesitated. "But the lady was very vague about whether these chickens are good layers, or even if they lay at all. They seem a bit young."

He hopped into the back of the wagon and dragged the big chicken crate over to the tailgate. Carefully he opened the hatch on top, peered in—and snatched. A brown hen came out squawking, her leg firmly in his grip. Expertly he flipped her and pressed her against his side with the crook of his arm. Her head stuck out behind and her behind stuck out ahead. She crowed long, hollow *grrrrrks,* but she didn't struggle.

"Give me your hand." He took hers in his and pressed her four fingers flat against the chicken's backside. "If you can feel the breastbone below your fingers, she's laying. If the space between her breastbone and her vent is less than four fingers wide, she's probably not making eggs yet."

"Then she's not laying yet. Wish I'd known that this morning. The lady had a whole flock to choose from. I could have picked out the chickens on a little better basis than just pretty colors." Polly flushed. "Actually, I *was* a bit more discerning than that. I looked for an alert eye and perky behavior, mostly. I tried not to choose sickly birds."

"You did fine. If these chooks aren't laying yet, they will be soon." With a practiced flick, he tucked the hen back in the crate. "Might want to turn them out into the barn a couple days until they get used to the place." He hopped to the ground and dragged the crate closer to him.

"You know a lot about farming. Grow up on a farm?"

He nodded. "Owned one for a while. That two-year drought dried out my soil and my profits, though. Bank foreclosed."

"You and your wife?"

"Never married."

"No wonder the bank foreclosed. It takes a minimum of two people to run a farm well. I've learned that much this last month. So you became a drover."

"Became a soldier first. Two years at Anzac. Egypt and the Dardanelles. Turks almost shot my leg off, so the army sent me home with a discharge. Then I became a sheepherder."

"Did everyone who went to Egypt go on to Turkey?"

"Not sure."

"And you never met a Chaplain Peter Chase?"

He shook his head. "Not surprising. Tens of thousands of Anzacs went over there, and I wasn't interested in religion then."

"And most of them never came back."

He paused a moment, carefully choosing words. "A lot died, or were mustered out. Others went on to fight in Europe. Some in Palestine. I hear Es Salt in 'eighteen was a real ripper." He smiled suddenly. "The army's a frugal sport, mum. They don't pay a farthing more than they need to. If your Peter had died, so would his paycheck."

The corners of her mouth lifted, but it wasn't a smile. "I'm sure. Still, it's hard sometimes, just waiting. Once in a while I wake up at night and can't remember what he looks like for a moment. That terrifies me. My biggest fear is that he'll walk up to the door and I won't recognize him. Wouldn't that be horrible?" She studied details of the chicken crate carefully. This was an

38

absolutely ridiculous time for her eyes to be getting hot; she really did not understand herself a bit.

He wrapped a long arm around her shoulder and squeezed. "You'll know him. He might gain five stone and grow a beard, but you'll know him."

"Of course I will." She snatched up the coffee and sniffed. "I wish coffee tasted the way these roasted beans smell."

"Or the whole chook tasted the way the crisp skin does." He swept the chicken crate up and balanced it on his shoulder. She watched him carry it off to the barn. He opened the non-sagging barn door with one hand and disappeared inside. The door closed.

Her imagination followed his movements. He would scatter hen scratch all around first. Now he would drop down to a squat and pop the crate hatch open. Sure enough; she heard the chickens cluck and gurgle. And now he would be standing up, taking care to rest his weight primarily on his right leg.

Only a few days ago she had noticed that he tended to favor his left leg at times, especially when he was tired. At last she knew why; a war wound. And his poor gashed arm had finally ceased seeping, but it was not yet truly healed. Then there was the theft of his horse and belongings. And the foreclosure—misfortune seemed constantly to be running over and jumping on him. He was such a fine man to suffer such consistently miserable luck.

She toted the coffee to the house. She ought to make some biscuits to go with the kidney pie. She pushed in through the kitchen door. The stove was hot now, the kettle beginning to warm up. Tea, soon.

You know, surely Colm Stawell could not be the perfect specimen of a good fellow that he appeared to be. Pleasant, polite, industrious—there had to be a dark side to him, a flaw or two. Or three or four.

She paused to inspect the pork chops she had purchased—tomorrow's dinner. She hoped he would like this special treat.

39

Flaws. Back to the subject at hand. For one thing, look at the way he had just stepped into this farm and taken over. He never asked permission to make repairs and changes. He simply made them as he wished.

And then a week ago, when he disappeared for three days and came back with eight yearling ewes and a ram—she didn't want any sheep. He claimed he traded them from some itinerant pastoralist. What if he was running stolen sheep in her paddocks? It could be. She'd thought at the time those sheep came much too cheap.

And, too, he must have walked all over her bed sticking those bits of paper up through the cracks in the roof. She bet he didn't take his boots off to do it, either. Next, he'd be talking about putting a ceiling up on those timbers and making it a proper finished room.

She put away the tinned oysters and baking soda. She had just hit upon it! There was his biggest flaw. He went his merry way and never considered her wants or preferences. He had no right to do any of the things he did. She was mistress of this farm; he had no portion here save as a sort of glorified watchdog. A self-appointed protector. Well, maybe she *had* hinted. . . . She spooned tea leaves into the pot. The water was almost ready.

Protector? All that day when he had ridden over to Maggie's, Polly had cowered in the house, almost afraid to go out and milk the cow. How cowardly. When he returned at dusk with Binta and the cow, he had said "No Maggie," but he did not elaborate. There was another flaw; he seemed reluctant ever to tell her anything. Maggie was her friend, not his. She ought to be informed about the poor lady. And that first night, she knew nothing about his infected arm until he pulled his coat off to lie down. *It's all very masculine to be a man of few words, but he carries the fetish much too far.*

The water was ready enough. She poured it into the pot. There was still another flaw. He knew too much to be a simple farmer. Or a simple drover. Or a simple soldier. Or a simple anything for that matter. And he had mentioned he was headed for Broken Hill to try mining. A simple miner next? Something had to be wrong with a man who drifted from job to job so frequently.

He came in the back door. "Can I help?"

She shook her head, handed him a cup of rather weak tea and promised dinner in fifteen minutes. He drifted off into the sitting room to flop in the chair with a book.

For no particular reason, she glanced out the kitchen window. It was getting dark out there now, the day ended. She saw her own reflection in the window, a dark shadow on the dark glass. Funny. She had never noticed that before. Her reflection peered in at her. It smiled, a bright toothy grin with an upper tooth missing.

She shrieked. She shrieked again. They were here! The men she feared most had come!

Colm came thundering into the kitchen. He glanced toward her and the window. He snatched the butcher knife off the drainboard and charged out the door.

Her knees felt rubbery. She tried to suck in air and could not. They were shouting out there like banshees. The hideous howls sounded almost like laughter, as if a troop of hyenas were tangling. She should run out and help Colm. Surely they were too much for him. She wheeled as the back door swung open. She shrieked again.

He was an Aborigine, lithe and quick and blue-black. His tan shirt stopped above his elbows and the cut-off dungarees ended just below his knees. Chalky gray-white powder dusted those parts of his spindly, scrawny legs and arms which extended beyond his clothing. His shirt was open halfway down the front, revealing the patterns of deliberate scars, the cicatrices that marked a man's initiation into manhood or something. Painted green-and-white half-moon marks extended down his cheeks. His hair, dark and curly, tangled around his neck and ears. He grinned again at her, that hideous grin with one front tooth gone.

He and his cronies had won the fight! They had bested Colm, who no doubt lay dead or dying out there. And now Polly was at the mercy of these beasts. Her knees melted and she plopped in a heap beside the stove, paralyzed.

Colm popped in the door behind the Aborigine, all cheerful. "Mum, this is David Kulg. . . ." His smile fled. "*Polly!*"

He reached her in two strides and dropped down beside her. Those warm, strong hands gripped her arms and lifted her tenderly to a chair. Her only comfort was his face. It told her in no uncertain way that he was deeply concerned about her.

She opened her mouth, but all it would do was breathe. She pointed, speechless, at the Aborigine.

Colm wagged his head. "Sorry, mum! Wasn't thinking. I shoulda come through the door first. David here is a cobber from 'way back in my cocky days." Gently he laid a finger on her chin and tipped her face toward him. "Hear me? A friend. A reliable, loyal friend. I trust him, and so can you."

She closed her eyes and drew in as much air as her lungs would hold. A friend. She let all that air out and looked again at the ash-covered cobber in her kitchen. "A friend." *With a face that doesn't show at night and a jack-o-lantern grin. The Cheshire cat with one tooth missing.* "Do you realize . . . ?" She closed her eyes again. "No, of course you don't. He's your friend."

Colm squeezed both her hands in his. "You just relax and calm your nerves down. I'll set a place for David and serve dinner up." He scooped her half-empty teacup off the drainboard and set it near her elbow.

She nodded numbly. A place for David. So this friend would be staying for dinner. Wonderful. Just "apples." Peter exercised a missionary's zeal toward the Aborigines in general, but he had never cared for them much as people. What would he say to feeding one under his roof?

Poor Peter. Perhaps it's as well you haven't gotten home yet. What you don't know won't hurt you.

CHAPTER 5

POLLY SAT UP STRAIGHT and arched her stiff back. It must be well past ten; her lamp was nearly dry. She craned her neck to double-check her guess against the clock in the corner and pushed away from her sewing desk. She looked over at the leather chair, expecting to see Colm fallen asleep. He was alert, though, reading intently with his lips pressing together, tucking in, pushing out.

His eyes still on the page, he reached out and scooped up *Smith's Bible Dictionary*. He plopped it on top of the Bible and thumbed to some reference, studied the dictionary a few moments, laid it aside and went back to reading. Polly admired long attention spans in other people; she herself could not read for more than an hour or two before she felt like leaping up and doing something else awhile. Colm had been sitting there studying since right after supper—a good four hours. Absently she fingered her own night's work and put her mental stamp of approval to it—quality lace and quite a long bit of it.

She stood erect. "Play the scholar as long as you wish. I'm done with the day."

Colm grunted. "Didn't realize it was this late. David hasn't shown?"

"No dead kangaroos on the porch."

"Then he'll likely come in tomorrow. Said something about going over to Maggie's place."

"Why would he do that?"

"I told him what little I knew about her disappearance. He thought he'd go look around, see if he can come up with anything. Just might, too. He can read the bush a lot better'n I'll ever be able to."

"Really! I got the distinct impression you could track a soaring eagle back to the egg it was hatched from."

He smirked and laid his Bible aside. When he stood and stretched, he filled that half of the room. "Might be gone myself early—check on the sheep and look around that west end a little."

"If you're thinking about sinking a bore out there, don't bother. I'm not drilling any wells until Peter gets back."

"G'night, mum." He disappeared into the darkness of the kitchen. She followed him out and locked the door, as always, behind him.

She snuffed the lamps on the way to the bedroom. She sat in the pitch darkness on her bed a few moments, thinking and dreading. She thought about the blouse she was taking off, a shabby thing without trim or frills. She wiggled out of her black skirt, half of her complete wardrobe of skirts. The other, better, black skirt she saved for town. This one was frayed at the hemline and she had mended already two rips where her heels caught in the aging fabric. She thought about the daring fashions in Wiggins's store in Corley, with their elevated hemlines and new colors. Her own frumpy skirts almost touched the floor. Exposed ankles might be scandalous, but they were practical for a farm wife always kneeling to scrub floors or weed gardens. But then, what farm wife would do chores in high-fashion dresses?

Make-up was acceptable for all women now, not just

actresses and harlots. Her own face was unadorned. Maybe she could make a new dress along the modern lines, perhaps spiff up a bit. A touch of color. . . .

Of course Peter was quite conservative. Would he want to come home to a painted progressive or to the good old demure wife he remembered? She had better stick with the demure look.

She slipped out of her camisole and into her flannel nightgown. Here came the dreaded part; she crawled between the covers. She despised this time of year. Her cold, clammy bed wrapped around her as an octopus attaches, sucking the warmth out and making her feet cold. She curled up in the blackness with her knees nearly to her chin, giving up as little warmth as possible to the chill, demanding sheets.

Colm's bed, a few blankets in the hayloft, was surely no warmer. She had doubted his motives at first, but those doubts had long since died. Never had he made any untoward suggestion nor had he sent any unseemly hints fluttering at her feet. What did he want here, exactly? Did he feel some obligation to her for helping him last April that he worked so industriously for nothing but meals and a roof? No one owed her that much. And now here was David, strange David, to complicate the picture. In a way, Polly wished they both would leave. She didn't like complications and things that might be beyond her control. At the same time she dreaded the possibility that Colm might decide to move on before Peter returned. And he just might, if David learned that whatever happened to Maggie posed no threat to Polly.

She shuddered, only in part from the cold. *Hurry up, Peter! I'm getting so tired of waiting.*

Something clunked in the kitchen. A possum? Mice? Polly's head launched off her pillow. She heard another sound, a quiet sound, as in a drawer sliding. The cold forgotten, she rose silently and jammed a straight-backed chair against the door knob. She opened the bedroom window slightly.

46

"Colm!" She screamed it loud enough to call down from the heavens any stars named Colm. "Colm! Hurry! Come!"

His voice came not from the barn, but from the kitchen. "I'm here, mum. It's all right. Just David and me."

"Colm? What are—?" She snatched her shawl off the bedpost and yanked the chair aside. She slipped out the door and tiptoed the length of the black parlor.

Colm had lighted a candle on the kitchen table. There sat David by the window, thoughtfully munching away at the leftover biscuits. An apple core lay on the table. David made fast work of apples. Colm stood by the cupboard. He had broken Peter's shotgun open and was peering down the barrel toward the candle. He started pawing through the cupboard drawer.

"I cleaned that drawer out last week. The shells are on top of the sideboard now."

"Mmm." He slammed the drawer—no sense being quiet any more—and groped around on top of the sideboard. "David thinks he can find Maggie, but he needs a little help."

"Sixteen-gauge help?"

"Better'n a spear for distance work. How many guns did Maggie keep around her place?"

"Just that one. What kind of distance work?"

"Long distance, if they have shells for Maggie's shotgun. They didn't have a gun of their own when they left me, if it's the same outfit. The tracks around Maggie's are pretty well blithered by now, but David found some good stuff up by the buttes—three men, later two, with a dog and a barefoot woman. They appear to be hanging around a billabong south of the buttes. You don't need Jewel for a couple days, do you?"

"I certainly do. I need her right now because I'm coming with you."

Colm's pockets bulged with shotgun shells. He

47

babbled something absolutely aboriginal and David grunted a three-syllable reply.

"David agrees. You shouldn't come. We'll only be gone a couple days. Maybe less. If the party isn't bush-rangers and the lubra isn't Maggie, we'll be home by daybreak."

David grinned, displaying all those pearly white teeth and the gap. "No worries. Home soon. Maybe bring Maggie visit."

"No worries! It's my horse and my shotgun and I shall accompany them and that's the end of it. I'll be dressed by the time you get Jewel saddled." Polly wheeled and raced back to her bedroom. She didn't trust those two; they would as soon slip away without her as breathe. She pulled on her blouse and skirt, snatched up her shoes and ran back out through the kitchen. She almost tripped over a gutted kangaroo carcass lying on the back porch.

She jogged across the yard to Jewel and leaned against the roan rump, hopping up and down as she pulled on a shoe. "How did you get into the kitchen, anyway? I locked the door."

"Through the window," Colm replied off-handedly. With a length of whipcord he was tying her water can to the saddle. "Oughta get you a neck bag for the horse. Carries water a lot better."

David's two dogs, both blue-gray-and-charcoal-brin-dled curs, cringed and backed away from her. Worth-less mutts. David stood near Jewel's head, casually leaning on a long spear.

Polly struggled with her other shoe. "You might have simply knocked, you know. The civilized thing to do."

"Thought you'd be asleep." Colm swung into the saddle and kicked free of a stirrup. With a practiced twist of the reins he brought Jewel around.

She tucked one toe in the stirrup and planned her next move. An iron grip seized her arm and yanked her up level with him. She scrambled onto Jewel's back behind the saddle and worried about her ankles showing. That was silly. Every woman from the Prime Minister's wife to the lowliest maid showed more of the leg than Polly was revealing now.

They took out across the yard in the blackness. David walked up beside Jewel's ears, covering ground as quickly as she did with his loose, gangling stride. His mangy dogs trotted in close beside him. Now and then one would range out to sniff at some dark thing, then return.

Polly regretted within minutes her decision to come along. Here was another of those many famous ill-considered moves of hers. It was not so much the discomfort of straddling bony Jewel. It was more the man in front of her. She soon felt secure enough to keep the horse's rhythm and cling only to Colm's belt. But the feeling of his bulk haunted her anyway.

There is an enormous, nagging difference between theory and practice; between the abstract—Peter—and the concrete—Colm; between the distant smoky memory of a man and this immediate, brooding presence which brushed against her with Jewel's every stride. She could feel his solidity, his masculinity, and it troubled her more than she could express. Peter melted into ever greater oblivion as Colm waxed closer and more real. She wanted to avoid touching Colm altogether—and at the same time she wanted to hang on for all she was worth.

David dropped back beside them here. He poked Colm's leg and jutted a thumb toward Polly. "You dance for her yet?"

"No!" Colm snapped, and his tone of voice added an unspoken "Shut up, David!"

"Dance?" Polly frowned. "You don't strike me as a man who would want to dance."

Absolutely delighted, David burst into rollicking laughter. Colm stiffened. Intrigued by some private little jest, David strolled a few steps forward and melted into gales of laughter all over again.

Polly snorted. "Doesn't take much to keep him amused, does it."

Colm chuckled and relaxed; she could feel his backbone loosen up. "Little cultural joke there. David figures if he laughs loud enough he'll chase away old Goolagaya."

David sobered instantly. He darted a quick dark glance at Colm and fell in close to Jewel's ears again. Obviously Goolagaya was a person to be feared.

"Who's he?" Polly asked.

"She—A twisted mythical old woman who snatches and eats any child who wanders away from the safety of the fire at night."

"Isn't David a little big for that?"

Colm shrugged. "You never know just how big she'll take 'em."

Here was a flaw in Colm she never would have suspected. He seemed delighted to cut his aboriginal friend with the knife of primitive fear and then rub salt in the wound. In one smooth speech he had both questioned David's manliness and played upon one of the poor fellow's greatest terrors. Not so obvious was that gleeful reference to dancing. Should Polly ask clarification now or wait until she and Colm were alone sometime? She chose to wait.

She chose also to walk. She spoke to Colm and slid off Jewel's angular rump. It felt good, walking—to a point. After several hours, though, Polly wanted most of all to crawl into that cold, clammy, oh-so-inviting bed back home.

They traveled awhile amongst low mulgas, spooky shadow trees. Eventually the trees gave way to scrub. A million arrow-sharp spinifex blades poked through Polly's skirt to scratch and stab at her legs. Her shinbones were going to be a pity to behold tomorrow— all red lines and dots, like a Morse code message gone berserk.

David stopped so suddenly Polly bumped into him.

He mumbled something. Colm replied in undertone. All Polly could see was blackness.

Colm laid a warm hand on her shoulder. "See that bright star ahead? We want you to walk toward it. If a gun goes off, lie flat on your stomach until either David or I call you or come get you. Understand?"

"Not a bit of it. What's happening?"

"Do what I asked."

With Peter's shotgun balanced across the pommel of his saddle, Colm rode off at an angle; the darkness swallowed him instantly. David jogged off in a different direction. His dogs, which a moment ago had appeared totally undisciplined, ranged out to either side of him. They were three hunters now, seasoned and hard and dangerously competent.

Polly stood coldly, frighteningly alone. That star twinkled chill in the late-autumn air. She wanted to shout. She wanted Colm's massive bulk close to her. Shaking more from fear than from cold, she started forward step by step.

What if she stepped on a snake? What if clouds covered her star? What if something happened to Colm and David? She had no idea in which direction home lay. What if—

Gray globs took shape in the darkness ahead. They reached higher and higher until they blotted out her guiding star. The ground tilted forward and away. Should Polly continue forward, down into this ghostly riverbed all lined with gum trees? She skidded down a loose slope and stood in river sand. A frogmouth flitted past her in a swooping arc. Without thinking she covered her head with her hands, though she knew perfectly well that the little whippoorwill-like bird would never tangle itself in her hair. She had lost her star. She slogged across shifting sand and tried to clamber up the far bank. She slipped back.

She stood still a few moments, listening. The leaves in the tops of these vast, gangling gum trees rustled ever so slightly. She saw a less-than-black mass to her right and reached out to it; she had this craving to reach out to anything at all. It was, as she knew, a gum tree trunk. She pressed her hand against it lest she be alone in this blackness. It's bark responded with no warmth at all—only coolness, smoothness, as if it were shaved and polished.

She tried again to climb the bank toward her star and failed. It was too deep here. She must go downstream a way, find a cut where she could get up through the loose dirt. She took four or five hesitant steps and stopped. No, this was wrong. To find a shallower, rounder bank she should be moving upstream. Banks tended in general to get steeper as one moved downstream.

She turned around and walked upstream five paces. The silence and the darkness stopped her like a wall. She was frightened. Not terrified, not panicky, not distraught—just frightened—and sometimes being simply frightened is more terrifying than terror itself.

Polly listened in vain for any reassuring sound at all. David, his dogs, Jewel, Colm—surely one of them would make a tiny little noise to tell her she was not alone in this empty black world.

Then the war started.

Far to her right downstream a shotgun went off, both barrels.

David's voice, banshee-strong, ululated in the blackness near her star.

Two other voices cried out, yelling to each other. Another shotgun blasted the stillness. Screaming, cursing, shouting, footsteps and hoofbeats all tangled together out there. The dogs of war engaged each other with horrible barking and snarling and yelping.

Polly ran upstream two or three paces and wheeled around. She raced back to her gum tree, cold as it was, her only friend. She shrank down behind it, wedged between it and the steep riverbank, cowering.

"That ain't no animal!" A gruff, thoroughly Australian voice came out of the darkness downstream. "Oy 'eard footsteps!"

Now what? Colm said nothing about this. It wasn't a gunshot, but Polly was seized by a sudden urge to lie flat anyway. She clamped her hand to her mouth and held her breath, fearful even that would be heard.

Aborigines do enjoy hollering across long distances; Polly had long known that. David called out again. Where was Colm? In all this Polly had not heard him. She felt sorely tempted to venture out looking for him. She was frightened for him much more than for herself. Darkness and this gum tree gave her a measure of safety, but he had placed himself in the thick of it—whatever "it" was.

What would Peter say about this whole hideous situation? What if Colm and David were killed or disabled? And what if Jewel were accidentally in the line of fire of one of those guns? She pictured Peter striding in the door, home from the wars, asking innocently, "So what happened while I was gone?"

"Well, about your horse: there was this drifter, and an Aborigine. . . ."

The shotguns swapped thunder. A dog yowled.

Were Peter to find himself in this mess (though she could not imagine Peter being so foolish), he would stop for long minutes of prayer. Polly ought to pray, for Colm if for nothing else, but Peter was the one on speaking terms with God, not she. Quite likely, Colm also could speak freely with God; he was certainly enamored of God's Book. Polly enjoyed no such close relationship with either God or man. The lack weighed heavily upon her, for she yearned desperately for a protector to be hovering close now.

David yelled again. Polly could stand still no longer. She slipped from behind her safe and solid tree. Footsteps beat rapidly toward her in the sand. She could see only very dimly in this failing light. The fellow approaching her was too small to be Colm, too wide to be David. He saw her, too. He hesitated only a moment, then lunged for her. Polly wheeled to flee but he caught her easily. His smelly arm wrapped around her and he began to drag her up the wash.

Polly could not stand the thought of being so close to this repulsive, unwashed ogre. It was almost as abhorrent as the thought of being a hostage, a pawn, a shield. She snapped her head back and caught him in the face. She began screaming. She kicked and flailed violently in all directions. She did her level best to bludgeon him with the back of her head. That failing, she shrieked. Even if she couldn't dent him physically, she'd ruin his ears.

He grunted and relaxed. He could be shamming; she dare not let up. His arm fell away, but she kept flailing wildly. She tried to run but the loose river sand slipped beneath her feet. Long hard arms grabbed her.

She tried to swing her head and kick, but the arms held her too close. The fellow used Colm's warm deep voice to tell her it was all right now. He pressed her closer. "Polly, Polly."

It took her a moment to sort friend from foe, so crippling was her terror. She sagged against him. "Who . . . ? Was that one of . . . ? Where is he?"

"Got away. Doesn't matter. You all right?"

She nodded. The gesture probably wasn't too reassuring, since she was sobbing now. She put the thought into words. "He didn't hurt me. I was— I mean, I am—scared, that's all." She lifted her head. "Maggie?"

"She's drinking your water can dry and she looks hungry enough to eat my boots. Otherwise, she's fine. Come on."

She was done with thinking. She let Colm lead her by the hand through the darkness to a ring of orange light downstream in the riverbed. She tried to rake her scattered wits back together. They flew to the four winds.

Behind a cove of boulders, David was blowing life into a neglected fire. His dogs stood close to his elbow. In the dim glow sat Maggie, gnawing greedily at some sort of greasy bone. Polly slipped away from Colm and ran to her friend. She hugged Maggie and was nowise ashamed of the tears in her eyes.

David muttered. "Animals. Worse'n animals. White-fellers worse'n dingos." His fledgling fire flickered and flamed high. He stood erect. Somehow in the melee he had acquired Maggie's shotgun with the taped stock. He broke it open as Colm handed him two shells.

"Want to take a prowl around, or shall I?" Colm was watching the blackness out there.

"Me." David slammed the shotgun shut with a flourish. Polly expected him to carry it off with him, but instead he laid it gently by Maggie's knee. His black face scowled angry beyond words as he turned on his heel and stalked off beyond the fireglow into the night. The dogs padded silently off to either side.

Colm hunkered down beside Polly and rubbed his face with both hands. "They must have killed the kangaroo long about dusk; it'd take that long to roast the haunch here. David's mad because they wouldn't let Maggie eat any. Fed the dog, but not her. Enjoyed watching her go thirsty, too."

"Oh, Maggie!" Polly reached out impulsively and rubbed the lady's shoulder.

Maggie waved her bone cheerfully. "Fine now. White-feller, blackfeller good friends. You, too." Her dark face darkened further. "Binta? Nitta?"

"Fine. At my place."

"Ah! Everything apples!" Maggie belched and wiped her mouth with an arm.

Polly giggled. "Glad your ordeal hasn't changed you. I love you just the way you are." She frowned at Colm. "Were these the—I mean, when you—?"

He nodded. "Same drongos. There's my swag right there."

"Where's your horse?"

"They ate it. Otherwise they probably would've taken Binta or Nitta. Came on Maggie near her humpy and decided having a lubra along might be fun. The pool of blood was one of them; she got him with her shot-gun. She says he died a fortnight ago of infection."

Polly shuddered. The whole business was too ghastly to dwell on. She watched the resilient Maggie a few minutes. Maggie was ready for anything. David and Colm were all excited yet, bucked up and rearing to go. No doubt they would return home yet tonight. Perhaps Maggie would come on to Polly's later to retrieve her animals. Or perhaps Maggie would simply stop at her humpy for a day or two of well-deserved rest. Or maybe Maggie would decide farming was not for her and go off on walkabout as she had so often threatened to do. Then again, Maggie might. . . .

Polly was done guessing. She was suddenly painfully weary. She didn't want to travel a yard further, and they were a good five hours away from home. She would force herself through the rest of the night be-cause she had to and because she did not want to show the world (more specifically, David and Colm) that this Aborigine lubra twenty years her senior was more fit than she was.

She could hardly wait to flop on that wonderful frigid bed and snuggle into her soft feather pillow.

Peter, you sure are missing out on a whole lot of excitement . . . you lucky rascal you.

CHAPTER 6

THE FOURTH OF JULY. Brass bands, fireworks, red and blue bunting, perhaps a clambake and almost surely a strong dose of warm summer sun. Summer? In a pig's eye!

Casting aside memories of warm Fourths of July long past, Polly pulled her wool wrap close around her ears, tucked her head forward and started across the yard with a pail of steamy milk. Cold pounding rain slashed at every bit of exposed skin; it drummed itself through the weave of her shawl to chill her shoulders. Her breath made smoke; they were just an ace short of having snow today. She almost would have welcomed snow if they had to have something. Snow doesn't wet you as thoroughly as this icy winter rain did.

She raised her head only after she reached the porch. She glanced back across the yard, all hazy gray from sheets of rain. Here came Colm in from the woodshed with a huge arm of newly split stovewood. He stomped up on the porch. His poor tired hat sagged even more in this wet. He pulled it off and shook it.

Polly spilled her milk into the funnelled top of the

cream separator. "The Fourth of July is the essence of summer, the pinnacle of school vacation—that's 'holiday' to you—and the reason there are marching bands and John Philip Sousa. This mid-winter-in-July is unnatural. Ridiculous. One good thing about the weather though, if you need something good to say about it, is that it cools the milk quickly."

"Cools the kitchen quick, too." Colm pushed in the door with his firewood. Polly heard it clunk into the woodbox beside the stove.

She walked inside, pulled off her shawl and shook it out. "My point exactly. Even what's good about this weather isn't really all that good. Where's David? I haven't seen him for days."

"Brought Binta and the cow in from the west paddock a few days ago and took them back to Maggie." He shook his own coat out and hung it on the peg beside the door.

"When we took Maggie home that morning—the night we found her—David was sticking to her like wallpaper on plaster. He seems to admire her quite a bit. Am I reading the aboriginal mind correctly?"

Colm wandered over to the stove, picked up the ladle and scooped himself some porridge. "Wouldn't be surprised if he did a little dance for her one of these days. She's twice his age, but that doesn't mean all that much in his culture." Colm was half smiling.

"There it is again." Polly broke three eggs onto the hot griddle. "What was that reference, anyway, about dancing for me?"

Colm sprawled out in the chair by the window, the place he had usurped from Peter. "The appropriate way to approach a woman—to suggest intimacy, you might say—is to do a courtship dance for her. She analyzes your dancing style and decides whether you're worth cultivating any further."

Polly wheeled, her mouth open. "What he was asking, then, was whether you—whether we—whether you and I . . . Why, the brass of that . . .! If I'd known,

I would have kicked his ear purple!" She turned the eggs over with a vengeance. One of the yolks broke.

Colm laughed out loud. "You have to remember his values are different from yours."

"You can say that again!" Polly scooped Colm's eggs on a plate, pulled two slices of toast out of the warming box beside the stovepipe and delivered the man's breakfast.

She broke her own eggs onto the griddle and stirred them with a fork. Scrambling was much easier than over-easy. She didn't feel like taking a lick more effort than she absolutely had to. In fact, she felt so crabby and short lately that she didn't care whether she acted crabby and short. She poured both coffees at once, retrieved her own toast and flopped into her chair.

She studied her eggs a few moments. Why were eggs a traditional breakfast food? Today, they made her half sick just looking at them on an empty stomach. "Since we're on the subject of David . . . exactly how long do you suppose he'll be here yet, anyway?"

"You sound irritated."

"He puts away a good twenty pounds of flour and potatoes a week."

"On the other hand, he brings in a hunderweight of kangaroo and goanna meat."

"That's another thing. Must he eat it raw?"

Colm just smiled and spooned in the last mouthful of porridge.

Polly snorted. "You're the most aggravating man on earth! You won't even fight fair!"

"Arguing's for married folks." He didn't look up.

She sighed and plopped an elbow on the table. She tucked her chin into the palm of her hand and stared out the window awhile. Eventually she spoke—just to hear a voice.

"I was talking to the banker last week, in town. He says the value of our place here is almost double what it was when we bought it, because of the buildings and dependable water." She waved a hand toward the window. "Notwithstanding that water falling all over the ground outside just now." She waited for a response. Nothing. She continued. "The reason the subject came up is that another fellow was inquiring to buy a farm. Family man, Scots-Irish, decent sort according to the banker. Fought at Ypres. Knows something about farming, too, from what I gathered. The banker suggested a leasehold, but I said no."

"Why?"

"What if Peter wouldn't want the arrangement? Once the lease is written up, we're stuck with it, and Peter would be bound to a deal he didn't like."

Colm straightened. His fork paused as his eyes met hers. "You have this attitude that you're a caretaker of Peter Chase's sacred property. You aren't, you know. You're an equal partner with Peter Chase. This place is as much yours as his, because marriage is a partnership."

"You sound like those suffrage people back in the States."

"Bible. Proverbs thirty-one." He polished off his eggs and paused to swallow. "Spells out the attributes of a good wife. She makes sure the house is in order, but that's not all she does by a long ways. You see, her husband is an elder in the gates of the city. Back then, people brought all their law stuff—law suits and land transfers, thieves and murderers even—to the elders in the gates to be judged. Or witnessed. Being an elder gave him fair dinkum prestige and immense respect, but no take-home pay! The only income mentioned in the whole chapter is the wife's. And she makes plenty."

"Oh, come! You're saying I should be supporting Peter? Honestly!"

"No, mum." Colm popped the last of his toast. "She makes girdles—that is, belts—just like you make lace. Exact same thing. Cottage industry. Course, that's all they had then, being no factories. She bought a vineyard, and no mention she consulted her husband, and she decided on planting it."

60

"But the New Testament says to be subject to your husband, and I promised to love, honor and obey."

"No suggestion she wasn't subject to her husband. He did his job and turned her free to do hers, so to speak. First time it mentions him, it says she does him good and not bad all her days. A man can't ask for more than that. And the last mention of her husband, he's praising her to the skies. So she must've been doing exactly what he wanted. Her husband was off serving God, just like Peter is, and the Proverbs wife kept the home fires burning, like you ought to be. But she didn't just sit on it; she built it up, buying land and making her girdles and developing the place. Extending their holdings."

"The Book's twenty centuries old. It doesn't apply to our times."

"It applies to every time—then till now."

"Where does it say she leased her vineyard out while her husband was gone?"

"And remember the parable of the good steward? The boss cocky gives him five talents and he doubles it. Gives another bloke two talents, and he doubles it. But the larrikin who sat on his one talent got swarmed all over. You could be doubling your investment. Livestock. Putting down a bore. Some dry crops. Sure the farm's value is increasing, but it's doing it on its own. You could be multiplying it, but you have to take a few chances."

"Yes, but I don't—"

"Step out on your own, instead of trying so hard to second-guess Peter that you don't do anything at all. You don't know if he'd approve or disapprove, so do your best for him—good and not ill all his days, including the days he's gone. When he gets home, turn it all over to him and step back. But until then, don't look to him to run the place."

"I don't believe this! Here you sit, a drifter, and tell me how to take care of my farm—and my marriage!"

"Just telling you what the Bible says." He glanced

out the window, took a harder look, brightened and rapped on the windowpane.

Polly knew without asking. David was back.

David came bounding in the door all grins. He was always all grins. Didn't his wind-up good cheer ever run down? His clothes were clean; Maggie must have been doing laundry; and they were drenched from his three-hour walk in the rain. Yet he didn't seem to be cold or shivering at all. He found his way, unaided, to the porridge pot and spooned out a heaping bowl.

"You look like a man in love." Colm tipped his chair back to two legs and sipped his coffee.

"Love?!" David snorted, but he didn't lose the grin. As he sat down in the third chair, he pointed to Polly. "You look like a woman arguing. Face all sour."

"My my. Aren't we all being refreshingly personal this morning. I trust Maggie's doing well."

"Too right." David nodded with his mouth full. "Talks she says go off on walkabout. Back to the bush. Up maybe Larrapinta, see her kids."

"She's always saying that."

"Maybe I go too, see what's up there. Been Oodnadatta once twice, is all." David waved his spoon at Colm. "Where you going next?"

The question shocked Polly speechless. Her mouth fell open. She could not imagine why it should punch her so hard.

Colm shrugged. "Ballarat maybe, now that their troubles seem to be over. Or maybe Broken Hill. Become a miner. Sound's interesting. Kalgoorlie's booming, but I don't feel like walking the whole Nullarbor to get there."

"Naw!" David's mouth full of porridge made his speech a little mushy. "No gold mines. Gold mines getting too deep now. Climb all day down, all day up, dig all day. Thass three days. Doan pay. Go dig opals. Not so deep, get rick quicker. No worries."

"Where's that?" Colm drained his coffee.

"Couple places. Coober Pedy."

Colm wrinkled his nose at the translation. " 'White man in a hole'?"

"Too right. Thass what we call it. They don't call it nothin', don't think. Why not 'Coober Pedy'? They dig in the ground like bandicoots, find their opals. Then they dig in the ground same way, make their houses. Under. Want another room? No worries. Dig one. Want a big parlor like city blokes? No worries. Dig one. All day all night in a hole. Good, too. Stays cool in summer, stays warm in winter. New leck-trishiddy, lots lights. No worries."

"Worth considering. Ever been there?"

"All way Coober Pedy? Not yet."

Polly searched Colm's face. His face told her very plainly now that yes—yes, he was seriously considering becoming an opal miner. And that was unusual, that his face should betray his thoughts, for it so rarely did. One impassive expression generally would fit any occasion.

But when he talked to David, his face melted in a host of expressive changes. Normally laconic, he would take off talking for hours—well, minutes anyway. That was not at all like him. He and David enjoyed a friendship of a most elevated sort. Whether in that aboriginal gibberish or in English gibberish with the Aussie accent, they babbled like magpies. They read each other's moods and interests well; they relaxed with each other. As with that rescue effort on Maggie's behalf, they worked together smoothly, like the parts of a well-oiled clock.

Polly felt vaguely cheated. She had not had that sort of a friend since her early college days back in San Francisco. Her best friend Mabel was married now, long gone to somewhere. Did Momma say Portland, Oregon? And her next-best friend hadn't written in years. She had no similar friends here; Eliza Belfour up at Magadura was a lovely lady, but they weren't close. Not like this. She had not realized her lack until this moment.

Even Peter did not give her this kind of easy friendship. They were man and wife, and quite happily so, but not true friends. How intensely she envied David!

Colm clunked his mug on the table. Startled, Polly looked at him.

"G'day, mum." He smiled. "We're low on stovewood. I'll take Jewel out and drag in some more. Maybe David and I might get in a little hunting. Anything you need doing around here?"

"No." Polly fought to return from her hazy thoughtworld. "No. I suppose you want the shotgun. Shall I pack you a lunch?"

He shook his head and stood erect. "No thank you, mum. We'll scare up something out there prob'ly." He scooped his coat off the hook on his way out.

David tipped his porringer to scrape the last of his breakfast up and hopped to his feet. He flashed Polly that flawed, brilliant smile. "Thank you, mum!" Like dark water he flowed across the room and out the door to join his friend.

Polly sat a few minutes, dwelling on David's tone of voice. It was exactly the same open, easy inflection that graced his speech with Colm. Freely and cheerfully, he was including her in the circle of friendship. She was Colm's friend; therefore she was David's, and he hers. It was so simple. And so profound.

But was she Colm's friend? She stood up with a sigh and wandered back to the bedroom. In her haste this morning she had left the bedroom a muss. She must put it back in order. Why must she put it in order? Because Peter might come home today. She recited the litany over and over, all the way through the house.

She paused in the bedroom doorway (a muss indeed!) and crossed to the dresser. She picked up that opal, that gift so generously given, and carried it to the window to see the fire again. She pulled the straight-backed chair over beside the glass and sat.

She had to hold the opal just so, for the rainy sky yielded its light grudgingly. The opalescent tints shifted in subtle ways, then shot out brief flashes of light. The gem gave her the strong impression that there was much more there she did not see than what she did see. She even turned it over to make sure she was missing nothing on the back.

She closed her hand around it. So Colm was thinking about becoming an opal miner. However he had come by this particular stone, it seemed to hold a certain lure for him. *Where you going next?*

David assumed Colm would resume his wandering ways, and why not? There was no future for Colm here, biding time on another man's farm. He had worked here willingly for months, receiving in return only room and board (and pitiful room it was, too; a few blankets in the hayloft). He and David had been watching for any sign of those bushrangers; apparently the fellows had quit the area entirely. Of course he would go on, for now it was time to go on. Polly was surprised he had not left already. *Where you going next?*

Coober Pedy.

An intense sadness wrapped around Polly's shoulders. It nearly suffocated her. It kept her from moving. It made her head so heavy she let it tilt over and rest against the clammy cold window glass. Colm would move on and Polly would sit here and wait. And wait. . . .

And wait. She shuddered a heavy sigh.

No. There had to be something better than waiting. She sat erect. What did he say? Proverbs. Proverbs thirty-one. She left the mussy bedroom behind, left the opal on her dresser, and went out to the sitting room. She sat down in Peter's big leather chair, the place Colm had usurped. She dragged the big Bible into her lap and opened it to . . .

. . . to . . .

. . . to the index. Peter and Colm were Bible students who could probably open the book precisely to any passage they wished. Polly looked up the passage by page number.

She was confused at first; the beginning verses said nothing about a wife. Ah, here it was. *Who can find a virtuous woman? Her price is far above rubies. The heart of her husband doth safely trust in her. . . .* Polly smiled. She liked the way this author thought already. The more Polly read, the more she could see herself reflected in the passage, although of course she had no children as yet. She did have rabbits and chooks and, thanks to Colm, sheep to care for. She milked the cow daily. Not the same thing, of course. She read on.

She sat back. Was Colm right? She lost track of time for awhile, thinking about her role as a wife and about the waiting, the endless waiting. Colm was right. She had essentially wasted five years. Oh, she had made yards and yards and yards of lace. In fact, she was turning out far more lace than anyone locally was rich enough to purchase. She had boxes of lace, just waiting for a purchaser. *Waiting*—that word again.

The woman in Proverbs didn't let her girdles collect dust on a shelf. She bickered with merchants until she got what she knew they were worth, verses 18 and 24. She brought her food from afar; did she carry her girdles afar to get the best price? Perhaps down in Adelaide or Geelong, Polly would get a better deal. But was it worth the cost of getting there?

She smiled to herself. Just listen to this! And only moments ago she would never have considered becoming a lace entrepreneur.

The Bible slid neglected from her lap and plopped all askew on the floor. Fearful for its binding, Polly lifted it carefully. A slip of paper fluttered to the floor. Curious, she picked it up.

The small, almost schoolboyish hand was not Peter's. These notes must be Colm's. They were Scripture references, chapter and verse. Nothing more. They were arranged in two neat vertical columns, so they must mean something as a group.

Deuteronomy 24:5	Proverbs 31:10-on
Proverbs 5:18	Proverbs 6:29
Prover (scratched out)	Proverbs 18:22
Ecclesiastes 9:9	Proverbs 19:14
	Ecclesiastes 9:9
	1 Corinthians 7
	Ephesians 5:22-on
	Colossians 3:18-19

What did Colm find so interesting? Intrigued, Polly laid the list on the table and looked up the first one, the Deuteronomy verse. *When a man hath taken a new wife, he shall not go out to war, neither shall he be charged with any business; but he shall be free at home one year, and shall cheer up his wife which he hath taken.*

Why in the world should Colm be struck by that verse? She tried the next down the column. *Let thy fountain be blessed: and rejoice with the wife of thy youth.*

She continued on, finding each verse, sometimes with difficulty. Colm must truly like Proverbs. She noticed 19:13 on her way to 19:14. Why had he not written that one down, since it spoke against arguing? He certainly did not like to argue.

It took a long while.

Finally, her curiosity not sated but rather piqued all the more, she picked up his list and simply stared at it. In this right colum were the instructions for building a happy marriage. Above all, they were warnings to faithfulness in the marriage bond.

And this other column, on the left? She drew a deep breath, startled. It was not a guide but a condemnation. Colm was assembling a litany of faults, and they were faults against Peter!

Peter should have stayed home a year with his bride. He should not have gone off to war. Peter had not rejoiced in the wife of his youth even in her youth. Polly scowled. It was none of Colm's business whether Peter followed the letter of some dusty old law, these vague and aged precepts. Why should they concern him at all? It looked almost as if Colm were weighing nearly everything he read in Scripture against this household—himself, and Polly, and the ghost of Peter Chase.

She never would have guessed such a thing of quiet, introspective Colm Stawell. And what use would he make of all this? Pick a fight with Peter? Upbraid him? Silently hate a man he never met because of some foggy supposed infraction of Scripture?

Peter, you really must hurry home quickly! Things are getting frighteningly out of hand.

CHAPTER 7

THERE STOOD JEWEL ACROSS the street, waiting as patiently as ever. Waiting. That word again. Polly despised making poor Jewel wait. Lately she hated making anyone wait. It was just one more symptom of a generally restless mood. She stepped out of the doorway of Wiggins's dry goods and general merchandise into the slanting noonday sun. Where next? She marched smartly down the street to the post office, the hem of her good black skirt flapping around her ankles. She stepped from cool sun to frigid gloom and crossed to the iron-barred window which protected her, necessarily or not, from the mousy little graying postmaster.

The old gentleman glanced up over his bifocals. "Ah, Mrs. Chase. G'day!" He pulled a small sheaf of mail from a pigeon-hole. "Letter here from San Francisco. Mmm. Five or six pieces this time. Makes it almost worth driving into town."

She smiled. "Thank you. Does your nephew still collect American stamps?"

"Aye, mum, and I appreciate your thoughtfulness."

"Happy to." Carefully she opened her mother's

envelope enough to tear around the stamps. She passed the stamps back through the window and sifted quickly down through her mail. She tucked it in her handbag; she would read it at lunch. Should anything require an answer, she would write it before leaving town. "Nothing from the army, other than Peter's check here?"

The postmaster chuckled. "Well now, when you wrote them that letter, 'twas only a couple months ago. Remember, it's got to go clear around the world to Europe, some army bureaucrat has got to pass it to two or three underlings, the corporal has to write an answer, it has to go back up through the underlings to the bureaucrat, and it's got to come back around the world. You can't expect it to take wings and fly."

"There's such a thing as air mail, you know." She laughed. "Of course, it costs a pretty penny, which is not the army's way."

"Coo! Tis not the army's way to spend an ugly penny, for all that. Nor the postal service, either. Thank you, mum, for the stamps."

"You're welcome." Polly turned and headed outside, suddenly eager for lunch, and eager to read her mother's letter. Momma's letters were always a triumph of the spirit. Even when Papa suffered gout and Cousin Charlie was injured in a logging accident and the dog died, Momma's letters glowed with good cheer. Mother and David had much in common.

Colm said he would meet her for lunch at the wagon. Here he came, half a block away, striding down the street with his coattails sweeping.

"Ah, Mrs. Chase, and g'day to you!"

Polly wheeled. "Mr. Hollis. How's the bank today?"

"Never better. Booming. All Australia's booming. If I may be so bold, I wish to invite you to luncheon at Armand's. Gentleman there I'd like you to meet."

"Why thank you anyway, but I . . ." Polly stopped because the banker's cheery face had instantly clouded over. She glanced behind her. Colm stood by her shoulder, looking neither threatening nor sinister. Yet he might as well have dumped a bucket of water on Mr. Hollis. Polly waved a hand. "Clayton Hollis. This is Colm Stawell, an old family friend. Mr. Stawell, Mr. Hollis."

"My pleasure," Colm rumbled, and he extended his hand.

The banker muttered something grudgingly polite and accepted the handshake. His face was definitely that of a man who could not bear to trust a stranger in a sheepherder's hat. He forced a smile toward Polly. "Of course, Mr. Stawell is welcome to join us also. Any friend of Peter Chase's is a friend of mine."

"Oh. Well, I. . . ."

"We'd be happy to," Colm injected.

"Splendid! About noon then? At Armand's." Mr. Hollis tipped his hat to Polly, nodded pleasantly as possible to Colm and walked away upstreet.

Polly waited a few moments until the banker was beyond earshot. "We'd be happy to, would we?"

"He's trying to cook up some deal, obviously. Bankers don't get rich taking folks to lunch for no reason. Might as well hear what he has."

"But I'm not interested in any deals. Really, Colm, I wish you would mind your own business."

"Got my business pretty well taken care of. How's your list coming?"

He had twisted her words so neatly she was momentarily at a loss for any more of them. She dragged her dog-eared list-of-things-to-do-in-town out of her handbag. "I didn't get the hardware yet. Horseshoe nails, ten-inch hinges, plate hasp. . . ." She squinted. "What's this you added?"

He craned his neck. "Adze head. Barn roof is in bad shape. If you want more shakes to fix it, we need a new adze to cut them."

"Oh 'we' do, huh?"

He grinned disarmingly. "Some of us do. Let me take the hardware part. Sold your lace?"

She thought a moment. He was pushy and smug and

71

irritatingly high-and-mighty, but he had a sensible business head, too. Should she ask his advice? She'd probably regret this later, but. . . .

"I have miles of lace, Colm, and no buyers. It's not that ladies don't sew or like to be fancy in this town. There just isn't that much money to spare for buying fancy work. You should hear what Mr. Wiggins offered, and Mr. Heavey's worse. Pennies."

"Ever try setting up some sort of distribution deal with retailers in the bigger cities? Big stores in Adelaide or Melbourne would probably pay you better wholesale prices than you can get here, retail. Kalgoorlie's growing fast. Geelong. Might even be able to handle it all by mail."

She perceiveth that her merchandise is good. . . .

"You might have something. I'll try that before I'll give my work away." She giggled. "You'll have me writing letters all over the world." The mirth faded. "But no answer from the army yet—about Peter."

"They'll get to your request in their own sweet time." When he said it it came out "th'r aon swate toym" somewhat, though not quite. Polly thought of C. J. Dennis's lengthy poem "The Sentimental Bloke," written all in the same thick vernacular Colm used so freely.

She ripped the bottom third off her list—the hardware part—and handed it to him. "Armand's then at noon, I suppose. Oh. You need money for these things."

"Plenty of money. Pounds of it. Armand's at noon." He turned on his heel and strode away downstreet.

Pounds of it? He possessed the two quid recovered in his swag, the last she had heard. Of course, two pounds would probably cover the supplies listed. Still, she hated to think of him using his own money for her purchases. Ah well. She'd sit down with him later over a pot of tea and make things right.

The morning went much too quickly. She had not attended to half the odds and ends on the list, which consisted almost exclusively of odds and ends—boot laces, a hair clip to replace the one that broke last week, pencils (they were down to stubs now)—dozens of picayune items. Noon came before she even thought about the grocery supplies.

When Polly came to town alone she simply bought a roll and a piece of cheese and picnicked under the gum tree by the smithy. Today she would eat in a restaurant, a mongrel little place with false pretentions of pure-blood. As Corley was growing, its sense of self seemed to be growing even faster. Having purchased a simple kitchen extension from a lady named Momma Thelma, Herman Schmetz decided Corley needed a fine and fancy restaurant like the big towns had. He modernized nothing in the kitchen, but he hung fancy lights in the dining room, changed the wallpaper from one of little flowers to one of big gaudy flowers, and replaced the checkered oilcloth table covers with real linen tablecloths. The MOMMA THELMA sign came down and a florid ARMAND'S went up, and he jacked Momma Thelma's prices higher than the new sign.

Polly didn't like that sort of thing much. She had eaten often in Momma Thelma's. She never frequented Armand's—until today, thanks to Mr. Hollis and Mr. Stawell. She was a good block from the restaurant door when she saw Mr. Hollis entering the eating place with a country-looking gentleman. The banker was clapping the farmer on the back and nodding jovially. What a chummy pair—the poor farmer.

Mr. Hollis, Friend of Farmers? Hardly! The clever Mr. Hollis put ads in the city papers, telling all those war veterans about the wonderful farming opportunities north around Corley Bore. He had land to sell them, too, at only twelve pounds the acre—land he purchased from failed farmers for two pounds the acre. There was nothing illegal in Mr. Hollis's many dealings, but there was nothing ethical in them, either.

All these years Polly had steadfastly refused to consider business with that conniver. And now look! She should have canceled Colm's quick acceptance with a good solid "No!" Instead she was letting him lead her into something she absolutely did not want. Polly's basic flaw had just surfaced again; in her imagination she did the perfect thing, when for real, she found herself doing the less-than-perfect thing.

She heard footsteps behind her and Colm fell in at her elbow. "G'day, mum. We'd better agree on what we'll call each other in there; is it first names or last names? How great a family friend shall I be?"

It had not occurred to Polly until just then that the rest of the world was looking at her and this man, and the rest of the world did not know their relationship was wholly and purely innocent.

"My husband is Peter to you and I'm Mrs."

"Right enough." He held the door for her.

For the first time she noticed how smoothly and easily he changed his posture toward her. At one moment he might be advisor or protector or even mentor; the next, he was merely an observer on the sidelines. And now he had instantly transformed himself into a formal escort meet for a formal restaurant like this. And a noble escort he was, too; she relished the feel of his presence beside her. He hovered at her elbow, bold and strong. At exactly the right moment he moved ahead of her to lead the way to Mr. Hollis's table. He held her chair as the two men stood, then draped her shawl over the chair back for her. And yet in all this there was no intimation that he was some lackey. He was a gentleman, serving his lady proudly.

Silly Polly. You're reading into his bearing a lot that certainly isn't there. And yet, it *was* there. She was not just imagining it. After Mr. Hollis introduced everyone around, Colm sat down at her right, casual and in command.

The gentleman across the table was August Kern, just arrived from Mt. Gambier on the south coast. He seemed a nice enough sort, cheerful and enthusiastic about life. The man was rotund, yet not in the least a flabby kind of heaviness, and fair-complexioned. His golden beard bordered on a reddish tint. He wore the

74

clothing of a farmer and the mien of Santa Claus. His fingernails were broken back to the quick, his hands all stained and calloused.

He and Colm hit it off instantly. They talked of raising sheep near Adelaide and putting in apple orchards near Geelong. Mr. Hollis, acquainted more with the commerce in Commonwealth Treasury notes, had little to add to the rambling dialogue about the fruit of the land. Several times he tried to interject a thought, but failed. Served him right! It delighted Polly when someone trying so hard and so obviously to manipulate others failed. Perverse Polly! She almost giggled aloud.

They ordered, lunch arrived, and still the chatterboxes rattled on. Actually, as Polly analyzed the conversation, Colm talked very little. He need only ask the right question to set Mr. Kern off on some highly informative and helpful reminiscences. He seemed quite interested in Mr. Kern's farming expertise.

". . . the opal fields. Up north."

The phrase snatched Polly's wandering thoughts by the shirt collar and dragged them back immediately to the conversation at hand. Mr. Kern was talking about the opal fields and Colm was regarding him with renewed interest.

Colm's eyebrows lifted slightly. "How many?"

"Four parties that I know of, though they might pick up some more in this area. A family and three single folks. Two men are left off mining from Ballarat East, and the young lady—a proper young lady, I hasten to add—" He glanced at Polly—"seeking a decent job. She's of the working class and has no family of her own. A bit intense at times, but a nice girl for all that."

"And all bound for the opal camp. To mine?"

"The two single men claim they're tired of digging other people's gold. The family is from 'way down south of Melbourne along the bay." Mr. Kern sniffed. "Said he couldn't scratch a living from his farm there. Tried fishing and couldn't make a go of that either. Don't know about his fishing, but if you can't earn a nice living farming in that area, you're no farmer at all."

"How long before they're on their way?"

"Couple weeks. They want to rest their stock and fatten up the horses here where there's good grass."

Colm pondered, his fork hovering over his plate. "Lot of money floating around up there, I hear."

"I imagine. If that's the life you want. They say everybody up there lives in holes in the ground. Neither sun nor rain down a hole." Mr. Kern shook his head. "Don't want it if I have to dig more'n a foot to get it. I'll stay with farming myself."

Colm nodded. "Farmer's the last to starve."

"And the first to freeze and fry, too." Mr. Kern laughed, an infectious and rollicking chuckle. "Like his land."

At last Mr. Hollis jumped in, taking the bull by the horns as it were. "Mr. Kern is keen on good land, Mrs. Chase, as you see. Now I was telling him about your place, and—"

"I'm not interested. I think I've mentioned that a million times or so."

"Now hear me out. A year's lease. Nine months' lease, if you insist. I urge you to try it. Because you don't have any stock animals—"

"We have sheep." Polly would never have guessed she would ever be happy about it when Colm came home with that little mob of ewes; but just watching Mr. Hollis's mouth drop open was nearly worth the price.

"Mmm. Of course you don't have water except at the house. . . ."

"Plenty for the house and livestock and garden. And we're thinking of putting down a bore on the west side."

"Yes." Mr. Kern looked like an old plow horse anticipating oats. His ears figuratively snapped forward. "So you're just getting started. How much of your land is arable?"

Polly licked her lips. She had no idea whether the number were zero or one thousand.

Colm saved her by chiming in. "Half acre garden plot, ample for a family and some sales in town on the side. Good tilth. Another four hundred acres along the bottom could go into barley safely. Put in the west side bore and you could probably till just about the whole place—at the very least, grow winter forage in the paddocks."

"Near the creek?"

Colm nodded.

"Wide enough to float corn down to the Murray?"

"Naw." Colm laid his fork aside. "But if a couple more people around here would put in barley and show there's grain to ship, Mr. Hollis here could probably sweet-talk the railroad into running a spur to Corley."

Mr. Hollis lighted up like San Francisco Bay on Fourth of July night. Colm might as well have suggested he could walk on water; Colm had just voiced the confidence that Clayton Hollis could whip miracles from the blue sky, rabbits from hats. It was precisely the entrepreneurial challenge that would appeal to a big banking frog in a tiny pond. From that moment on, noted Polly, Colm Stawell could do no wrong in Clayton Hollis's eyes.

Mr. Kern was nodding thoughtfully. "You have a lot of faith in the area."

"It's a coming place, aye, Mr. Hollis?"

"Indeed, Mr. Stawell! Booming. Land values have doubled and they'll double again 'ere long. Farming is just getting started here, and as you know, Mr. Kern, farming is the backbone of any area's development." Mr. Hollis turned to Polly. "Mrs. Chase, Mr. Kern's wife suffers from dampness and cold, forcing him to move north into warmer climates. He's a farmer of the first water, and he desperately needs affordable land in time for spring planting, or the whole year is lost to him. Spring is hard upon us, as you know. Now I've told him a little about your place and it would be perfect for his needs. Even if you and your husband decide eventually not to sell, he can make a maximum return on your land investment this season—to the profit of both. Surely you see the wisdom in this."

Polly smirked. "I see a way to bring Peter through the door tomorrow—and that's to sign an irrevocable lease today."

Colm spread his hands. "As I know Peter, he'd prefer to settle in closer to town here anyway. He'd surely rather put his experience as a chaplain to use than to farm. There's not much in Corley in the way of churches. Wide open field for a man of religious bent."

Polly fumed. *As I know Peter* indeed! But she had to admit it was clever. Colm sounded just like a family friend, automatically stamping himself as a proper escort. He knew Peter, of course, only from Polly's wedding picture on the wall by his chair and by what she had said about him. And yet he was correct. Peter had purchased the farm through opportunity and not through any love of farming. She fumed hotter. These men, all three, were manipulating her—Mr. Hollis in bungling obvious ways, and Colm very subtly so. What made her angriest—it was working.

Mr. Hollis beamed expansively. "Let me bring Mr. Kern out tomorrow for a look-see. We can talk a blue line, but unless he sees your place with his own eyes, how can he pass judgment? And with his knowledge and expertise, he can at least make some helpful suggestions." He shrugged. "Even if there be no business transaction, a farmer always likes to look at prime land. Aye, Mr. Kern?"

"That's true." The beard spread out, stretched by the smile behind it.

Polly sputtered something on the order of "Well, I suppose so," but the true answer in her heart was "No!" She did not want this sidewinder Mr. Hollis crawling around on Peter's farm. Sidewinder. That was the word. It hadn't passed her mind in years. There were poisonous snakes aplenty in Australia, but no rattlesnakes. She could probably call the man a sidewinder to his face and he'd be none the wiser.

Colm laid his knife and fork across his plate. "Suppose your four wagon travelers would mind another traveler along?"

"Why they'd welcome you! Especially if I'm able to end my journey here. I'll tell them you're interested."

Colm nodded. "You'll see them this afternoon?"

"I will."

Colm dug into his pocket. "I trust ten pounds will show I'm interested. Would you drop this off to them, tell them I'd like to buy in?" He sorted two five-pound gold pieces out of his change and handed them to Mr. Kern.

Polly gaped and closed her mouth quickly. Where would Colm have gotten such a fistful of money? Mr. Kern wrote him a receipt, they chatted some more, and Mr. Hollis looked like a gladiator who had just come out on top in the arena. Polly went through the mechanics of politeness as they topped the luncheon off with tea, smiled a lot, exchanged pleasantries, and at long last went their separate ways.

Hurry, Peter! You're running out of time. I don't know if I'm going about this wisely or if my ignorance will cost us everything. I need you.

Colm is going away.

CHAPTER 8

POLLY CLIMBED UP INTO the wagon seat and twisted to look in back. There were the groceries, her miscellaneous purchases, the hardware, some parcels Colm had bought apparently, her accumulated issues of the *Bulletin* picked up at the news agent's—everything on the list was there. Well, everything available in Corley's limited shopping area, at least. The Corley stores never had *every*thing on her list. Still, something seemed to be missing. She twisted back around to the front as Colm clucked to Jewel. The wagon lurched forward. Was it Polly's imagination, or did Jewel respond better when Colm was driving?

The wagon rattled northward out of town along the rutted road. Polly wearied quickly of winter, for it ruined roads already none too good. An overcast sky was crowding the sun back. It would probably rain tonight, and quite possibly before they reached home. The end would be in keeping with the day.

She glared at Colm. "A superb performance today, Mr. Stawell. Applause, applause."

He turned to her and those soft gray eyes made hers flick away to study Jewel's ears. "Lunch?"

"Of course lunch. Twisting Clayton Hollis around your finger; do you realize what a black-hearted, despicable person he is? A conniver. He'll get a nice tidy fee for arranging this leasehold, you know. Mr. Kern seems somehow to have mistaken you for a gentleman farmer of means. And your clever little attempts to force me into doing something I'm against. . . . It was all so very smooth. And where did you get all that money, anyway?"

"Sold my saddle."

She gasped. Her head snapped around to search the back. That was what was missing.! He had brought his saddle this morning and now it was gone. "But why?"

"Don't need it. Next time I supply my own transportation, it'll have a motor and drink petrol."

"Really. Going to muster sheep with a motor car?"

"Stations supply horses. Don't need my own. You know, you might want to sell your sheep to Mr. Kern. He'll pay half again the price they cost you, especially with seven of them in lamb, and still be getting a good deal."

"You're so dead-set that I'm going to lease to August Kern. You and Mr. Hollis. Your high-handed attitudes and tactics make me mad."

"Good. Get your blood flowing. There's more to life than sitting around waiting with that blank look on your face."

"A blank—" If the buggy whip had been much closer she would have whacked him one. "Just who do you think you are, anyway?"

He smiled more to himself than to her. "Y'know, I just figured that one out myself recently. I'm a servant of the living God, bought into His service with His Son's blood, the most precious thing in heaven or earth, and I've been healed with His stripes. Since I belong to Him now, He takes care of me—on earth and in heaven both—and my job is to do what He wants. It's so simple I kept missing it, 'till I read Paul's letters more carefully."

She was speechless for a moment. "And what am I? Are you your sister's keeper?"

He shook his head. "I don't think you're a sister yet. But that doesn't keep me from wanting the best for you; maybe prodding you a little toward something better."

"Prodding?! I have never seen such an egotistical, condescending—" Polly stopped her ranting. She knew her speech was simply running off his back, like rain off the roof. He never took up the gauntlet, never responded to her tirades. *I don't think you're a sister yet.* Was that all he thought she might become to him? A sister? Of course! That was all propriety would allow her to be. She was another man's wife. Apparently he kept that in mind every moment. Not only that, in a way he kept Peter's best interests in mind as well as hers, even though he had never met the man, even though he held certain vague scriptural faults against him. Polly disliked confusing complexities, and the more she saw of Colm Stawell, the more confusingly complex he appeared.

Was that a shout from afar to the right of the road? Polly peered off to the east. Beside her, Colm stood up to search beyond the trees. A man shouted again. She could see him now, standing near some wagons in a shady little mulga grove.

Colm hauled Jewel aside and started off across the flat dirt toward them. "Looks like Mr. Kern's group."

"We're going to be home past midnight or so as it is. Let's not tarry long."

"Yuh, mum."

The man was indeed Mr. Kern. He had changed into stained, worn work clothes and now looked much more like the man he really was. He hailed them as they approached. All smiles, he waved a hand toward the wagons behind him. "I gave your earnest to Myers, Mr. Stawell. He's fair pleased to have you along. Since you're by, you might wish to meet your fellow travelers here. "G'day, Mrs. Chase!"

She nodded in return.

Colm brought Jewel in beside a rather fancy little red wagon with yellow trim. "Only be a minute." He passed Jewel's lines to Polly and hopped to the ground. He followed Mr. Kern off through the trees to a campfire in the distance.

Polly felt uncomfortable. Why? Gradually she realized she was being stared at. The back of her neck prickled slightly. She twisted in the seat.

A young woman leaned casually against the far side of the red wagon gazing at her. The girl was less than twenty, slim and almost boyish. She wore no make-up, but her dark eyes and rosy cheeks didn't really need any. Short auburn hair lay in finger curls around her ears. She came walking around the end of her wagon with a loose and swinging stride. Polly saw with a shock that the girl was wearing trousers.

They weren't the ballooning bloomers ladies sometimes wore as they rode bicycles. These were baggy woolen men's pants pulled tight around her thin waist with a length of rope. Her shoes were men's work shoes, her shirt plaid flannel.

She sauntered over to Polly and extended her hand. "G'day. So you're traveling with us to the opal fields. My name's Louise Flett."

Polly was about to correct her. Only Colm was going north with them, but a warning bell rang inside her head just in time. Cautiously she offered her right hand. "Polly Chase."

Louise grabbed her hand and shook with a grip that could crush diamonds. The girl frowned. "Chase? I thought his name was—" She licked her lips. "Can't tell a book by its cover. You and I should get on well. I'm not too hidebound myself. Live around here?"

"Yes. It's my farm Mr. Kern hopes to lease." Was the girl a conniving vixen or an artless child? Polly could not decide whether to loathe her or tenderly take her aside and explain about the fine use of tact.

"Oh, yuh? Kern's been babbling on about it like a magpie and he hasn't even seen it yet. Must be quite some place. Is it really yours? In your name? I mean, it's not his, is it?" She dipped her head in Colm's direction.

"No, it's not his by any measure."

Wagging her head, Louise smiled appreciatively. "Boy, I really admire that! Carving out a piece of the world for your own. Y'know, I'm gonna do that one day. Just watch. Buy my own land. You're smart to lease it. It's still yours that way. Course, even so, there's some things you still need a man for."

Here came Colm. Polly was never so glad to see him! On second thought, she was not so sure. Louise turned on her heel to face him. Instantly the girl's voice changed from firm and commanding to soft and mellow. "So you're Colm Stawell. Louise Flett." They shook and Polly wondered if Louise's grip was as devastating when she took Colm's hand as it was when she took Polly's.

"Pleased, mum." Colm smiled politely.

Mr. Kern stood by Jewel's head. "Well, that's all of us. I think you'll have a pleasant journey northward. Seems like you have a lot in common. Glad I happened to see you out on the track there."

"'Preciate your cooee, Mr. Kern." Colm settled into the seat beside Polly. "Have a good evening, Miss Flett." He nodded toward Louise.

She smiled, all teeth. "Mrs. Chase, Mr. Stawell." "Mr. Stawell." She gave his name just the least little extra emphasis. Polly could not see that Colm had noticed anything, but she sure did! Artless child? Alley cat!

Colm dragged Jewel's head around and they were on their way again. Polly did not look back. The myriad wagon-rattles disturbed the silence. Nothing else stirred. The wheels crunched through little clumps of spinifex and over broken mulga branches on the ground.

84

They bumped back out onto the track, but the road was hardly smoother than the open country.

Presently Colm sank forward until his knees supported his elbows. Jewel's lines hung slack and casual in his hands. "Y'know, mum, there's the place to sell your lace. Those two miners I was just talking to—Myers and Hargreaves—they're of the notion that the opal fields are full of wealthy men looking for the good things of the world, and the good things are slow about trickling into the bush that far. You could get retail, and top retail at that. Sell every inch of lace you have."

"It's a thought." Polly could not force her mind to abandon Louise's memory. Why should she care whether the girl lived or died, whether the girl noticed Colm or any other man? That child-woman in man's clothes fascinated Polly in a way. She was unique, a female of the kind Polly had never met before. Louise stepped out and took responsibility for her own actions, obviously. There was probably very little disparity between Louise's world of imagination and her real world.

Louise's attitude both intrigued and revolted Polly. What hurt most was that Colm would travel hundreds of miles with that—with that provocative creature. Since Colm had no wagon of his own, he would ride with others, and she was one of the others.

Polly toyed momentarily with the idea that this was jealousy eating away at her, and nothing less. Tosh. All tosh. Colm said not long ago that he wanted the best for Polly. Well, the reverse was true. She admired Colm as a person and she wanted the best for him, too. And she could not for the life of her see Louise as being the best for anybody at all. It wasn't jealousy at all. It was concern.

Colm seemed wrapped in his own thought world. To keep awake, Polly climbed in back and dug out her *Bulletins*. She clambered back into her seat. The *Bulletin* was a weekly, so Polly got to receive four copies each time she went to town. She thumbed through each in turn, interested mostly in Alfred George Stephens's commentaries. The problem with holding a degree in literature was that there was so little you could actually do with it. Now if she had earned a diploma in, say, tax computation, or practical farm management. . . . But literature?

Despite Alfred Stephens and the *Bulletin,* Polly fell asleep all melted against Colm.

"We're home." His voice brought her, groggy, but awake, back to reality. It was a cold reality; she shivered.

"What time is it?"

"Gone two in the morning, I'd guess."

She sat erect. Every bone in her body ached from being scrunched down like that. "I'll unload if you'll milk. You milk faster. Want anything to eat?"

"If you don't mind at this hour. I'm pretty hungry."

"I laid the fire before we left. When was that?" She climbed to the ground, still stiff. "A week ago? A fortnight?"

"Century or two." Colm unhooked Jewel's traces. "Glad Mr. Kern hailed us up there, though, to meet those folks."

Polly took a grocery crate along and stumbled to the house. She was starting to wake up now. She glanced off beyond the buildings toward David's humpy and saw no fire there. The next few minutes would tell whether he were around at all; the smell of cooking would bring him in from a hundred miles off.

The kitchen was colder than a grave and the stove slow to get going. She lifted off a plate and pulled the stewpot directly over the open flame. She'd probably burn the bottom of the stew, but they'd eat a little quicker. Polly wanted to end this day as fast as possible.

The darkness hung heavy. Even when Polly lighted two lamps, the kitchen gloom weighed on her. So Mr. Hollis was bringing Mr. Kern out tomorrow because Polly had given her permission. Mr. Hollis was so terribly anxious, in fact, that he was bringing a prepared picnic. That meant they would leave town extremely early and be here not long after noontime. Polly wished she could sleep the whole day away, to make up for the twenty hours she had just spent on a wagon or on her feet. As Colm pointed out and as Polly already knew, Mr. Hollis must have some sort of bonanza to realize from a lease deal. And Polly was letting it happen. She could just kick herself.

She heard milk sloshing in the separator as she laid two dishes out. Colm was leaving her, practically on the arm of that auburn-haired floozy. Polly could just cry. Of all the women in the world—

Colm came through the door with his arms full. As always, his presence filled the room, even when he stood to one side of it. He put down the last of the grocery crates and whipped a box out from under his arm. He handed it to her unceremoniously. "Saw you looking at this in the window this morning. For when Peter gets home." He disappeared back outside.

Polly hefted it on the way to the table. It made the tantalizing soft sound of fabric rustling amid tissue. It didn't quite have the weight of a dress. In her hurry she broke the twine with her bare hands.

Reverently, carefully, she lifted it from its protective tissue. Yes, she had looked at it in the window of Wiggins's dry goods store—not just this morning, but a month ago and the month before that. It was the black dress for late afternoon or evening in the most modern style. The fabric hung smooth and flaccid with a charming drape. The yoke and front were trimmed in swirling ropes of black sequins—tastefully lavish. This dress was not the sort of thing Polly would ever wear. She admired it only because she dreamed of wearing it. There is a difference. What would Peter say?

Her eyes got hot and started to brim over. Suddenly she clutched it to her, scooped up the box and ran to her bedroom. She threw the box on the bed and quickly wriggled out of her plain blouse, her weary black skirt.

How good was Colm at guessing sizes? She dropped it over her head and wrenched her arms around to button up the back.

She was afraid to see herself. It took almost more courage to take her first look in the mirror than to face Peter with this on.

She liked what she saw. Oh, she liked it! Colm had guessed almost right; it was a bit large in the waist. But this may well have been the closest available size. Wiggins's selection was limited. She pulled the shoulders up closer to her neck, studied the effect a moment, and pushed them back down where they ought to be.

The neckline swung wide from the shoulders inward and took its time reaching the midpoint in front. She turned a half circle and looked over her shoulder. The neckline plunged just as deep in back. A black folded satin rose drew the eye to the fashionably low waistline. The hemline licked at her shins. It was tastefully uneven, higher in the front than in the back. Ah, yes. There were her ankles, just barely, in all their flagrant exposure. This would definitely take some getting used to.

She heard the kitchen door close. The stew must have stuck in the pot; the iron pot lid clanged first on the stove, then on the floor. Colm had smelled the stew and burned himself removing the lid to stir supper, and dropped it. She took a deep breath—several, in fact—and crossed the dark sitting room into the kitchen.

He had popped the butt of his right hand into his mouth as he stirred the stew with his left. He turned, gazed. The right hand drifted downward forgotten and Polly could see the red mark on it. His face widened into a smile at once both boyish and manly.

He purred, "Better'n any man deserves."

Suddenly embarrassed, she studied the scuffed wooden floor. "I'm still uncertain whether to accept it. It's so much, and—well, it's so very personal, too, and—"

"You're too sensible a woman to buy a sequined dress to wear in the bush feeding chooks. That's a virtue in a woman. And you'd never spend money on yourself when the black skirt will do. That's a virtue, too. So I took it on my own. For Peter. If there's a vice, it's mine." He ripped his gaze away and turned his attention on the pot. "Stew's hot. Sit and I'll serve."

Obediently she sat. Suddenly she hopped up, pawed through the sideboard bottom drawer and dug out two of her good linen napkins. She laid one at each place and sat down again.

Colm asked a blessing—something new, and in a curious way welcome to her. They ate in silence. She attributed the quiet to the fact that he rarely talked and she was much too tired to. On the other hand he seemed preoccupied—not quite worried, really, but unsettled somehow. Was he regretting his purchase-gift? Would it be polite for her to offer to reimburse him, or would it be an affront? Eventually she voted for affront.

She stood up when she finished, scooped seconds for Colm without asking, and prepared a pot of tea. Then she simply sat and watched him awhile until the silence got too thick to bear.

"So you met your traveling companions today. What do you think of them?"

"Rather unusual bunch, all of them. But then, the usual folks all stay put in one place."

She giggled. "I take it, then, you count yourself among the unusual."

"Well?"

She nodded. "However, you're not staying put because of your string of bad luck. I suspect you'd very much prefer to simply settle down in a nice circumstance and raise a family and be—" she waved a hand— "usual."

"Too right! More than you know."

"Speaking frankly—I presume this is a time to speak frankly—I regret seeing you go. I appreciate your help around the place here. It's in much better shape than when you first came. I realize now a woman alone out here should have some protection. Maggie's incident showed me that. And I appreciate your good company, too, more than you might guess. I don't mean just someone to talk to, though heaven knows I bend your ear enough. I mean just having another human being around, even if you're out in the paddock worming the sheep while I'm in here churning butter. I didn't realize how lonely I was until you eased the loneliness."

He half smiled. "Enjoy listening to your accent. You pronounce all your vowels wrong."

"Yes. Of course. But understand, I can see that there's nothing for you here, really. The moment Peter gets back, you're on your own. Adrift again. And nothing to show for all your months of work here."

"Maybe I should stay around. Protection."

"You and David say those two are long gone. No tracks, no trace."

"There's others in the world." He shook his head. "I owe you for helping me when I needed it." He held up his right arm and wiggled his fingers. "Nice getting the use of my right hand back. Thought for a while there I was gonna be cacky-handed for good."

She shook her head. "No, don't stay. This is the perfect opportunity for you. The opal fields are one of the few places in the whole world where you can start with absolutely nothing and build a comfortable living. Perhaps even a fortune. No initial investment, such as a farm or station requires."

"Not many come away with a fortune."

"No, but many make decent lives for themselves. That's what you want."

"You're sure?"

"Am I wrong?"

He smiled and wagged his head no. "Was thinking along those same lines myself."

"Yes. Well, I've been thinking a lot, too. I don't know what you Aussies call it, but in the States it's called a grubstake. A person of means provides the miner or prospector with money to live on—food and such—and in return gets a share of whatever wealth the miner happens to unearth. If the prospector finds nothing, the mentor is out his investment. If the prospector strikes it rich, so does his mentor. It's an exciting way to invest. Adventurous. Much more fun than stocks and bonds."

"Prospector. Fossicker?"

"I think so. Anyway, if you're going fossicking, I would like to grubstake you. It's an investment and it's also a thank-you for your months spent here."

"The thank-you's enough. Don't need money."

"I know that. I said 'investment' and I mean it. They say that to be successful in the opal fields you have to be out digging twelve hours a day. You are industrious by nature. You aren't going to drink your profits away or waste them to some foolish fancy. I'm convinced you'll do well—that my investment is sound."

He pushed his dish aside and sat forward, both elbows on the table. He laced his fingers together and studied her, his lips pushing in and out. "With this stipulation. If Peter feels it's a poor investment, we cancel the agreement and I pay you back somehow."

She grinned. "Deal!" and extended her hand.

He enveloped her small cool hand in his warm massive one. He shook, not nearly so grippingly as Louise, but he did not let go for long moments. He let his hand slip away. "Come with me."

"What?"

"I don't mean in an immoral sense. I'm not making an unwholesome suggestion. But come along up to Coober Pedy. Sell your lace. If you lease to Kern, the trip will save you money because it'll be a couple months you don't have to pay rent on anything. If Peter gets here while you're gone, Mr. Kern can tell him what's going on and he can be the one to do a little waiting once. Won't be that long. And you can make a tidy profit with your lace. Come back with lace money,

91

lease money—a fine nest egg to start again with Peter closer to town."

She looked closely into the smoky gray eyes and forgot any objections she may have had, were there any to have. "I'll think about it. I haven't said yes to that lease deal, you know. I'm not sure. Colm, am I taking too much responsibility? All these decisions?"

"Just multiplying your talents. Besides, every decision looks pretty big to you if you haven't been making any at all for a while."

She laughed. "Thank you. You are my conscience and my guide."

"Scripture is your conscience and your guide. I'm the middle man, since you haven't been reading it much."

"I should change that, shouldn't I. Read the Bible more."

"It'd be good."

"Then I shall, starting now." She sat back shaking her head. "I can't imagine that I spent five years sitting. Vegetating. Reading my literary magazines and puttering along from day to day. I could have been growing. Stepping out. I used to in college. My first year at Stanford didn't bother me a bit. You know the old speech they give you about 'This is a major step in your life.' "

He shook his head. "Never got through school that far. Finished grammar school, though."

"It's nice, a college degree, but not the key to happiness. Then Papa was offered a temporary position at the University of Adelaide. It sounded so utterly distant. Not to him, of course; 'utterly distant' to him is the fringes of the galaxy. But I didn't want to hold back. I was all eager to go."

"So you finished your college education in the University of Adelaide."

"Yes. It's funny. We were years there, and I don't know anyone in the city. I was all wrapped up in school, with only a few chums who've moved to the four winds

92

now. Momma puttered in her garden and hardly ever entertained. And as soon as I met Peter, I didn't socialize much with the general crowd. Anyway," she waved a hand, "I never had trouble making decisions or taking major steps, as they say. And then . . . I don't know."

"So you changed. Was it the book-learning, the marriage, or the waiting?"

She studied him, thinking. "The waiting. I'm certain of it. It was so easy to just turn into a vegetable and sit, waiting. I let the waiting drag me to a stop, I guess. And now I'm afraid to run. I'm frightened. What if I do something very wrong? Lose money or lose the farm? It's so easy to make a mistake, especially when you're dealing with that banker, Hollis."

"Anyone who takes responsibility puts himself at risk in some way. Risk is part of it. You consider all the risks you can think of, do what you can to minimize 'em, and then wade right into it, boots and all. Same as the servants with the talents. The two good servants couldn't double their master's money without taking a few chances. The bad servant wouldn't take the chance."

"I suppose." She sighed and closed her eyes. The late hour—rather, the early hour—was weighing her eyelids down. "Thank you," she murmured. She forced her eyes open. "Thank you for this dress. It's just lovely. And thank you for being here. Just . . . just thank you."

Words, for all their charm, are sometimes inadequate.

He looked at her for the longest time with those smoky gray eyes saying nothing that she could read. Suddenly, his voice strangely hoarse, he bolted to his feet. "Time to go. See you tomorrow. And lock the door." He strode quickly across the kitchen and pushed out the door into the blackness.

She pressed her hand against her mouth, trying to trap inside her some emotion she could not even identify. It escaped anyway. Her churning, confused thoughts swirled all hollow in the empty kitchen. The stove was cooling off and the kitchen getting cold again.

Oh, Peter! This is a horrible thing to say, and I'm so sorry: but for a moment there I almost wished you weren't coming home at all.

Please, please hurry to me!

CHAPTER 9

AUSTRALIA AND CALIFORNIA. Were California ironed
out flat, they would look perhaps a bit more similar.
But as both stood now, there was no similarity at all.
California's magnificent Sierras, her Range of Light
(to quote John Muir), buckled upward thousands of
feet. Australia's Flinders Range stretched ho-hum
across the flatland, a rambling, easygoing assortment
of mesas and rolling hills. No one born in California
would ever call them mountains. It seemed almost that
the hills of Polly's San Francisco were steeper than
these mountains.

And the flats . . .! Not even the Pacific Ocean looked
this flat. Polly recalled with a shudder the storms that
sent waves breaking over their steamer's prow forty
feet above water line. Now and then a line thicker than
the pencil-thin line of the horizon would mark a forest
of low mulgas, or the gum trees lining some distant
billabong. Horizontal lines. All horizontal.

Polly leaned back in the wagon seat and closed her
eyes, wearied of watching all the horizontal lines.
Wherever you are in your life, she mused, you can
never possibly imagine where you'll be going a year

hence, or five years hence. Five years ago at age twenty, Polly was completing her degree and marrying, within three months of each other. At age sixteen she was beginning that college career; it had seemed a big step at the time, but it was really just a short pause in her life. At age twelve she watched San Francisco go up in flames in the aftermath of the quake. At age six, hardly realizing what she was seeing, she watched the world celebrate a brand-new century. Fireworks then, the fire in aught-six making night as bright as day, the fiery phosphorescence in the wake of their Australia-bound ship, the brush fires up behind Adelaide that frightened Peter and her on their honeymoon trip, and now the quiet crackling campfires along this north-bound track.

Coober Pedy.

White man in a hole.

She was falling asleep. She sat up straighter and glanced at the white man in the wagon seat beside her who soon would be going down a hole in Coober Pedy—or digging one.

"It's so quiet. And so horizontal." She spoke her thoughts aloud.

He nodded.

"When we were coming over here—when Papa was coming over to fill that temporary chair at the University—I was told all sorts of things about Australia by my college friends. I use the term *friends* loosely here. Mabel was all for it. But the others; you should have heard. Australia was full of murderers and cutthroats, the dumping ground for all England's riffraff. It was absolutely covered coast to coast with black-skinned sub-human natives and strange little inferior animals and all manner of weird plants. It was a hostile continent; that's what an acquaintance in Early Tudor History called it. Can you imagine thinking of David as a sub-human?"

Colm smiled. "David's way ahead of us in a lot of ways. He has his family history memorized—totems

96

and all—back twelve or fifteen generations. I don't even know who my father was. He can look at bare ground and tell you what man passed through two weeks ago and what the fellow had for breakfast. He can stand in the middle of this country—the kind white folks call an empty desert—and live comfortably. Food, water even when there's no open water for a hundred miles. We're the sub-humans."

"He go with Maggie?"

"Probably caught up to her. I think she left about a week before he did." Colm shrugged. "See? Trackless waste, so to speak, and those two will get together as if they planned to meet on such-and-so street corner."

Polly nodded. "Maggie tried to show me some bush tricks, and I guess I'm just too dense to understand. You picked up some from David."

"Not much. Not compared to what he knows."

Polly watched Jewel's ears awhile. "This is all happening too fast, Colm. Mr. Kern visits the farm on a Tuesday and by Friday the lease is in hand. He seemed to know about raising rabbits. You do think Muffin will be all right, don't you?"

"Too right. And I think you're making the right choice to bring Jewel along up to Coober Pedy. She's getting old. Look at the gray around her muzzle there. Flea-bit on her rump."

"She's always been flea-bit. It's the roan in her."

"Gotten worse just since I've been around, half a year. She's getting too weak to do farm work and August's horses are young and strong. If you want, you can almost certainly sell Jewel and the wagon at the opal camp and take the train back. Or a mail truck. They'll probably have a jitney service sooner or later, too."

"She is getting a little decrepit." Polly watched the graying ears flop listlessly. Jewel was twelve when they bought her and that was. . . . Mmm. Polly had not noticed how old Jewel was getting. "Did you see Mrs. Kern's face when we left? She actually had the garden spade in her hand, ready to go to work. She just loves gardening. I think they'll like the place very much."

"Seems a good match—Kern and that farm."

"And I can just see Peter walking in the door the day we left. This could be a lark, or a profitable business trip, or a disaster. Maybe Peter won't bother coming for me. We were only together four months." She turned to Colm. "Does that mean I have eight months left to be a bride, or am I already an old married woman of five years?"

He chuckled. "Suppose it all depends on how old you feel."

"Truck coming!" Mr. Pitts at the rear of the train called out.

Polly twisted around to watch. Louise's rig was directly behind, and the Pitts wagon beyond that yet. A dusty tin truck chugged toward them. It pulled alongside the Pitts wagon and a man in the truck seat shouted back and forth with Mr. Pitts. The Pitts's horses did not like trucks a bit, especially nearby trucks. Mr. Pitts pointed toward Polly.

Here came the truck on by. It pulled abreast Polly's wagon and the driver hallooed.

Colm shouted above the ridiculous racket of the truck engine. "That a Jeffrey Quad?"

"Yuh!"

"What year?"

"Fifteen. And it's a beaut! Polly Chase?"

"That's me!"

"Package here for you."

Colm pulled Jewel out of the track and Louise rattled on by. Polly hopped down. The truck engine rumbled and purred so violently the whole truck vibrated. The driver clambered up into the back and sorted through boxes.

"Army truck, four wheel drive." Colm patted a fender. "Nice piece of machinery."

"Delightful." Polly had secretly wanted to own and use a motor car for ages. But she was not about to let

98

Colm know that. Why did she feel so fickle? She didn't understand, but then she didn't really care, either. A package?

The driver jumped to the ground. "The postmaster at Corley said I'd come along you here. Here's your mail, too." He handed her two letters and gave the big parcel, a square over a foot by a foot, to Colm.

Colm asked a few more questions about the truck and the driver was off up the track again. Within minutes he had passed the rest of the emigrant train; in a very few more minutes he was but a white poof of dust at the apex of the road.

Polly climbed back into the seat. Colm plopped her parcel in her lap and clucked to Jewel. They would probably not catch up until the rest of the party stopped for lunch.

Polly surveyed her mail, happy as a child at Christmas. "The letters are from Eliza Belfour and my mother. The parcel is from"—she turned it around—"Mother also."

She struggled with the string. Colm loaned her his pocket knife. Success comes of having the right tools, obviously. She cut the string and dug in through the paper and box.

"Books! *National Geographics* and two books! What a thoughtful gift!"

"Happy birthday."

"My birthday's in February." Polly ripped open her mother's letter and scanned it quickly. "It's a no-occasion gift. Momma mailed it on my birthday so that it would arrive—here's how she phrases it—'When things are a little slow and it's not quite spring yet.' Isn't that thoughtful!" She read her mother's letter again, slowly and carefully. She read the letter from Eliza, which said essentially nothing but was wonderful to receive anyway. She examined the books lovingly. That was one thing she regretted—leaving her books behind. And yet, August Kern said it was fine with him that she should leave the library intact until

99

she returned. It saved putting them in storage and the danger to books that storage always poses.

It was nearly lunchtime. Her stomach said so. She looked over at Colm. He was practically in a state of repose, his feet on the dash and his elbows on his knees. It occurred to her that he had not once received a single piece of mail in all the months she'd known him. Here was a man without roots, and yet a man who so deeply desired roots. She could tell. It was a pity, in a way.

Eventually she put aside the books. She was getting very hungry, even feeling a bit cross. She hauled her muslin sack out from under the seat. She might as well redeem the time, as Peter often said. She brought out her lace-making bolster. She reached into the bottom of the sack briefly and let her fingers rub across the smooth face of her opal. She laid the sack aside and balanced the bolster on her knees.

Carefully she untangled the bobbins and laid them out on the bolster's velvet skirts, two by two. The wagon's right wheels skipped sideways into a rut, and all twelve front bobbins did a little dance over each other and executed unrehearsed double twists at random.

She sighed and sorted out the new tangle, bobbin by bobbin. "I don't think this is going to work too well. The light's so good, but the bobbins think they know the pattern better than I do."

"Take up crochet." His voice was flat and out of sorts.

"What makes you so ropable?"

"Nothing."

"Try again. What makes you so irritable?"

He shifted his shoulders in a pallid imitation of a shrug. "Mad at myself for talking you into coming."

"You don't like the company."

"The company's grouse. I'm doing you a disservice."

"I'm an adult perfectly capable of taking responsibility for myself. That's what you said, remember? And I decided to come on my own."

"Still. Doesn't look right."

"*Now* you decide it doesn't look right? We're as far from civilization as a human being can get and suddenly you discover something doesn't look right. I admit, from time to time I wonder if I'm doing rightly. And if I was still sitting at home I'd be wondering exactly the same thing."

"Not what I meant."

"Look right to whom? These people? There isn't even a cover on the wagon here, as you may have noticed in the last downpour. Here we sit in this open seat like shags on a rock for all the world to see. And in the evenings you hang around with Myers and Hargreaves and sleep at their end of the camp and I sleep over here in mine. What doesn't look right?"

"Forget I mentioned it."

"Peter's not going to shoot you, you know, if he comes to retrieve his bride and chide her for her foolishness."

"Even so, maybe I ought to travel with one of the others."

Polly cocked her head, instantly on alert. "Louise, maybe? I know for a fact that she's invited you into her parlor there more than once. I overheard her. She has a whisper that can call in hogs from Victoria."

Bemused, he studied her eyes. "You sound jealous."

"Jealous? No. I worked that out already. Concerned. I can see that you would be happiest settling down with a good woman who will take good care of you and mend your socks and raise the kids. And believe me, Louise is definitely not that woman."

"She's young and strong and pretty. She'll make a good miner's wife."

"She's conniving and devious. If her hooks were out any farther, they'd trip her horses. I've never been able to understand how an otherwise intelligent man cannot see when he's being bamboozled and played up to by some conniving woman. You men always just waltz into that kind of trap without a second thought.

It's an amazing phenomenon."

"Proverbs five. Or seven. Or both, I think. The loose woman's wiles, and their dangers. But Louise isn't loose. She's proper."

"There, you see? Blind as a fence post to her machinations. Haven't you noticed that when she first met you she was dressed like a Woomera drover? And since you joined up with this train, she's been wearing skirts every day?"

"Wearing skirts isn't proper?"

"You understand my point. Stop trying to twist my words around. She's putting on a front for you. Those billowing skirts aren't the real Louise. The raggedy men's pants with the rope for a belt—that's her."

"Practical, if you're working."

"I'm just saying it shows what sort of person she is, what she wears. And when she wears it."

"I still say you sound jealous." His voice had a little tickle in it. He was quite obviously enjoying all this. Polly began to get the vague feeling that she was being baited; that he had his opinions all firmed up and was simply drawing her out.

Her impatience and anger were boiling to the surface faster than she wanted. "Heed my warning or not, as you wish. She's a conniver, and connivers can never be trusted. And believe me, I'll take great delight in crowing 'I told you so!' if you fail to heed me."

Colm was smiling. It was the look of a man who clearly held himself superior in his skill at reading human character, male or female. For the first time since she met him, Polly saw on him a condescending smile, and it infuriated her.

She wrenched around in the seat to face him squarely. "I'm trying to point out in you a blind spot you happen to share with all the rest of the males in the world. I mention it only for your own good, and you aren't taking me seriously at all. You think you know better. Well, you don't. You're misreading the little snippet. You deserve whatever you get!" She twisted front again.

His face lost that superior smirk. "She's a nice girl, who's been through a lot of rough country, same as I have. She's trying to make a life for herself, and hasn't got much to make it with. Same as me."

"You like her, in other words, and nothing I can say will put you on your guard."

"We share a lot in common, and she's going north for the same reason I am—we all are. To try to do better for ourselves. Yuh, I like her well enough."

Come and get me, Peter, and hurry! I'm afraid Colm is going to make a dreadful mistake and I don't want to be around to see it when it happens.

CHAPTER 10

THE RELENTLESS SUN PUSHED itself through the little open spots in the weave of Polly's straw garden hat. The big brim cast a sun-dappled shadow across her book. Colm's sleeves were rolled up above his elbows and his arms were as toasty brown as his boots. The sunburn on Polly's nose itched. Late October got hot at the farm, but this was ridiculous. The sun heat poured down from on high and bounced up from the barren dirt all around them. She was surrounded like a chicken roasting in the oven.

By the channels of coolness the echoes are calling,
and down the dim gorges I hear the creek falling;
it lives in the mountains where the moss and the sedges
touch with their beauty the banks and the ledges.
Through breaks of the cedar and sycamore bowers
struggles the light that is life to the flowers;
and softer than slumber, and sweeter than singing,
the notes of the bell-birds are running and ringing.

Perhaps this is why she loved literature so much. Literature could transport you away from reality to whatever unreality you chose to experience. Channels of coolness, dim and shady streams, moss and flowers—what an absolute contrast to this sun-drenched flatness all around them! She chuckled out loud.

"Finding jokes in a poetry book?" Colm asked.

"No joke, believe me." She re-read the passage aloud to him. "Henry Kendall, written about fifty years ago. He's a native Australian, born in the bush. I like the imagery and the feel. Anything cool."

"I like the rhythm."

"You'd love Robert Browning, then. I'll try to find 'How they Brought the Good News from Ghent to Aix' for you. The whole poem proceeds at full gallop for page after page."

"'Preciate it. I'm not much for—" He stopped speaking. He was gazing out across the blank wilderness. He stood up to see better. He braced two fingers against his teeth and whistled. Jewel jumped, startled. Polly heard harness jangle on the wagons both before and behind. Colm waved his hat in wide sweeping arcs, watched a moment longer and sat down again.

"Who? There's something out there away off in the distance."

"Recognize the shirt?"

"I don't even recognize the species this far away. It must be a mile or more. An Aborigine, isn't it? Two or three." She squinted in the brilliance. "That can't be David, can it? Out here?"

Behind them, Louise shouted, "Who's that? Friend?"

"Good friend, yuh."

"Do I get to meet him?"

"Too right. Marry him if you want; he's unattached."

Colm settled back to his original elbows-on-the-knees position. His face was mild, at ease, betraying nothing of his thoughts.

Polly stared at him. "Now there's a side of you I've never seen before. You're being snide to Louise, teasing her, and she doesn't even know it. That's most unlike you."

"She'll catch on eventually."

"And how often do you tease me that I don't catch on?"

He turned and looked at her in an odd way. The gray eyes smothered her face. He opened his mouth to speak and closed it, then returned to his original study of the backs of Jewel's ears. Why did he give her that puzzled look? Or was it puzzled? Polly was very poor at reading emotion, if any, in people's faces, and Colm's face, especially, masked his true feelings. He had developed this remarkable skill, whether he realized it or not, of hiding behind those luminous eyes, of somehow putting them like glass walls between Polly and the thoughts she so much wanted to read.

She returned to her poetry book, her new book from Momma, but she could not concentrate. Colm's presence beside her bothered her. She could feel him there even when she neither touched nor looked at him.

She forced herself to think of Peter, and, like an errant child, the memory evaded her. It hid behind a haze somewhere—Peter, as seen through a glass curtain—and she could not bring him into vivid focus. Her own husband, and she could not clearly call up his face in the window of her mind. That made her angry, angry at herself and angry at Peter for not renewing her memories before now.

Joe Pitts called out from the rear of the train, "Truck coming!"

A distant hum accompanied a tiny poof of dust. The hum and the poof grew together into, respectively, a roar and a cloud. Jewel thrust her head high and rolled her eyes.

A large truck came bouncing and bounding by; its dust roiled up around poor Jewel. John Myers up ahead disappeared momentarily in the gray cloud. Polly craned her neck to watch as the truck got smaller and smaller.

She glanced at Colm. He, too, was craning his neck

to watch. He settled back absolutely starry-eyed. "There I go, someday."

She snorted, unimpressed, and tried to blow the yellow-gray dust off her book.

An hour later Ian Hargreaves called from up front, "Truck!" But the truck was not approaching from the north. It was the same vehicle they had watched so raptly an hour before.

It was perched atilt beside the track, its near-fore axle elevated on some sort of post device. One of its two occupants was struggling on his back with some sort of problem under the front end. The other man was buried up to his elbows under the bonnet, tipped nearly upside down. Ian spoke to them and the fellow under the hood came up for air and shook his head. The wagons passed on by slowly, raising very little dust.

Polly had a hard time keeping herself from looking up. "There you sit someday."

Silence. Long and enduring silence.

Polly started to doze, the shadow of her hat brim bobbing. Jewel stopped.

Ian called out from up ahead. Directly behind him, John Myers stuck his head around his wagon canvas. "Natives, Stawell. Up ahead. Might want something; they're standing in the middle of the track." He hefted his rifle where Colm could see. He was stopped, too.

Louise came driving up alongside and pulled her team to a stop. "What's up there, you know?"

"Not yet." Colm hauled Jewel aside and pulled out around John's wagon. Polly was amazed that he could manage to avoid locking hubs. Her initial observation was correct; Jewel did respond better for him.

Colm drove up beside Ian Hargreaves's wagon and handed the lines off to Polly. A hundred feet ahead of Ian's wagon stood David and two old Aborigine gentlemen. Polly was disappointed that Maggie was not with them. Perhaps she was close by. Colm would find out, surely, if she was.

David wore his shirt open and unbuttoned. The engraved cicatrices covered the whole front of him. He had wrapped a rag around his hips, dungarees gone. Polly wondered if the modesty were inherent or a function of his contact with whites. The two old men beside him wore nothing at all, except for the little tufts of kangaroo fur. Half a dozen brindled dogs, all so alike that Polly could not distinguish David's two, milled around at the men's feet.

Colm had reached the three now. David was grinning broadly with that Cheshire smile. They all nodded and babbled. The two old men each carried a long spear, but David had apparently traded his spear in for Maggie's shotgun with its taped stock. Obviously, David and Maggie had met somewhere in this vast expanse of nothingness.

One of the elders pointed east. Colm shook his head and pointed north. Louise brought her rig up beside Ian on the other side.

Ian wagged his head. "You wouldn't read about it! He even talks their yabber."

Polly aimed her reply past Ian to Louise. "Colm and David are cobbers from a long time back. David's not married yet, either."

If looks were daggers, Polly would have been shredded like sauerkraut. Louise, even when she wasn't glaring furiously, bothered Polly somehow.

David motioned toward Polly and spoke, laughing.

Colm punched David's arm in a gentle, friendly way, turned on his heel and came back to Ian. "The only good water is a billabong about five miles off the track to the east there. The next dependable water is north about thirty miles. David and his friends here have been down from the Larapinta; he's not too familiar with the area, but the two elders are."

Ian stood up and looked at the wagons parked behind them. He grimaced. "If it was just us, I'd say keep going north. But you think we might ought turn aside because of Pitts? His water barrel's low and his horses aren't doing well. Any grass?"

Colm shot a few fast words over his shoulder. One of the elders waved an arm in two directions, neither of them north.

"John, whaddaya think?" Ian twisted around to look at the other erstwhile goldminer.

"Probably ought to turn aside. But then, that ten miles would put us a third of the way up the pike to the next water. Let's go ask Pitts. Come on along with me, Stawell." John hopped out of his rig and started back to the Pitts wagon. Ian wrapped his lines around the brake and followed.

Louise kicked her dash in disgust. "Isn't anyone gonna ask me?"

Nobody did.

David came striding over to Polly's side. How did those slim, spindly legs move so many miles so fast? Polly noticed a traveling bag slung over his shoulder.

"How's Maggie doing, David? I trust you've seen her."

"Tellin' the whole world 'bout her 'venture." David grinned as wide as always. "Fluffin' proud of it, since she survived it."

Polly giggled. "I can see where she wouldn't be too proud of it had she not survived. You're carrying her shotgun. She never did like that gun too much. Rarely used it."

"I like it good enough. Spear? One barrel." He waved the gun. "Two barrels. She didn't want carry her gun, I say 'I take it.' So now I got that and her baby."

"Her *baby!*"

David skimmed the inside of his shoulder bag with one hand. Out came a puppy, a gray and squirming ball of fluff. He offered it. Polly cupped her hands and David laid the puppy in them.

"Isn't he precious! It's been years since I snuggled a puppy." She drew it in close, cuddled its warmth, scratched behind its ears. "Where did Maggie get it?"

"Didn't yet. Takin' it to her." David waved the shotgun toward one of the slinky, brindled-gray dogs beside the road. "That's the momma. My hunter, the good one, he's papa. Two best dogs in the clan. Maggie been missing a dog since she lose hers last year. This one's perfect for Maggie, think?"

"I agree. She needs a good one. She's trained more than one hunting dog, too. She's perfect for the puppy also." Polly frowned. "Only one?"

"Only one left, yuh. Brother dog went to my sister's boy. He's coming age now, needs a good dog."

Polly held the warm fluff-ball out and David reached for it. Long arms snaked out and whipped it from both their grasps. Louise stood at the wheel of Polly's wagon and gathered the puppy in close to her chest.

"It's so cute. Strange, isn't it, that something this adorable grows into one of those." She nodded toward the dogs by the roadside. She took a step closer to David, but she held onto the puppy. "How much will you sell it for?"

"Sell it?" David frowned, as if it had never occurred to him that one might buy or sell a dog, like merchandise.

"Not mine. Maggie Minnanong."

"I insist. I heard you; this Maggie doesn't even know it exists. You can get her another one. Hey, look. I need a good dog. Protection, help. This one has some sheepdog in it, I bet. Brains."

"Good dog, yuh. Sell, naw."

"Yes you will." Louise's voice took on a hard edge, a menacing tone. The threatening inflection in her voice was so at odds with her physical appearance that the sum effect might have been comical, were it not a bit scary.

David reached for the puppy and Louise tried to twist away, but he was too quick. He latched onto the little dog and bodily hauled it out of her hands. "Not mine. Maggie. Will be when I give it to her. Maggie needs it live good." He put the pup on the ground.

110

Instantly its mother picked it up by the scruff and carried it off.

Louise was staring at him.

David ignored her pretty much. "Warreem—he's my sister's boy—he says the little brother dog too smart already. Not even weaned yet, he thinks it hunts. He eleven winters old. What does he know?"

Colm came climbing up over the wheel. He settled into the seat beside Polly and took up the lines. "Relationships mean a lot in David's culture," he explained unbidden. "When two people meet, or a person joins a group, they find out first whether they're related and, if so, how. Their relationships determine how they behave towards each other."

"Are those two men relatives?" Polly nodded toward the other two.

"One, uncle. Other, just good friend."

"This is embarrassing." Polly felt her ears get hot. "But it never occurred to me that you might have relatives. Not even when Colm mentioned you can recite your family history. Isn't that dreadful?"

David laughed out loud. "My relatives? Wait'll you meet Maggie clan! Whole clan funny-kind people." He asked Colm something in his own tongue.

"Pitts's horses need the rest," Colm replied.

The two elders had already moved off toward the east. David whistled in the mother dog, scooped up the puppy and strode away through the spinifex, flowing along as effortlessly as running water on those long skinny legs.

Louise wandered back to her rig. Ian started forward and hauled his team aside to the east. They were on their way again.

"David mentioned Warreem. Warreem is David's sister's boy. That makes Warreem and David special. In some ways the uncle in that relationship is more important to the boy than the father. Same relationship that one older fellow there has toward David."

"Mmm." Polly glanced behind. "Colm? Did you

notice Louise's face and voice? Something unsettling in it. It's not—It's the way she acted about the puppy."

"You still down on Louise?"

"But there was something wrong, the way—" She glanced at Colm. "Oh, never mind. Either you heard it or you didn't. And since you didn't, there's no use trying to explain it. Are you sure we all ought to detour five miles off the track?"

"Sounds more like three and a half to four miles at most. We'll pick up the track in a day or two again. Not that big a detour."

Polly sighed and settled her hands in her lap. What if Peter should come up the road looking for her? He had no way of knowing she was off beyond the black stump somewhere, miles from the main road. He would blithely continue north, missing her completely.

Peter, after sitting so patiently five years, here I am gallivanting all over. I'm afraid to go and determined not to stay and wait. It's so difficult. Why couldn't you have returned six months ago?

CHAPTER 11

VIVID ORANGE, THE SUN hung a few moments above the low, flat ridges to the west. It squashed itself together a bit, then began its leisurely descent, dragging the darkness across the sky behind it. Polly paused near the wagon with her water pail to admire the changing colors of the sky. She scanned the northern sky and found Altair, but then she knew where to look. The milk dipper in Sagittarius just barely showed in the smoky blue overhead.

The show was too good to miss. Polly turned the empty bucket over and sat down on it. Louise came by a few minutes later. Already the sky was nearly dark and more than just the bravest stars showed. She looked at Polly, looked at the sky, looked at Polly again.

"Why you sitting here?"

"Watching. Looks serene up there, doesn't it?"

"I don't see much moving."

Polly smiled. "It's not serene. Apparently it's chaotic. The reason it doesn't look busier is simply that we're so very far away from anything else."

"You an astronomy amateur?"

"I suppose so. My father is a professor of

astronomy. The earliest memory of my childhood was being dragged out onto the hillside behind town to look at stars. Papa made sure I could pronounce Betelgeuse before I could say Paulette clearly."

"Yuh?" Louise squatted beside Polly's bucket. "Lot going on there, huh?"

Polly pointed. "That bright star in the north is Altair, the brightest star in the constellation Aquila. Aquila is the more or less A shape."

"Right-o."

"June a year ago, a star brighter than Fomalhaut there appeared in Aquila." More pointing. "It reached maximum and then faded gradually over a period of several months. So my father and several others went back through photographic plates. The day before it appeared so bright, it was a sixth magnitude star; that is, about as bright as that one." She picked out a dim marker in Capricorn. Keep it simple. "And a few days earlier it had been a star too dim to see without a telescope."

"Whacko. An exploding star."

"Exactly. Called a nova. Then this last January Papa photographed it again, very carefully, and they're finding a little ring of gas expanding out from it. You can't see Taurus this time of year, but they've found a similar gas cloud there also. There are several."

"You went to school, didn't you. University. It's the way you talk. I don't mean your funny accent. I mean the words you use. You a teacher?"

"No. Although I suppose that's about the only thing you can do with a degree in literature. What I am is a farmer's wife who reads."

"But not that farmer."

"No. Not that farmer."

"So what's the other farmer say about you two running off?"

Polly engaged in a quick short fight with anger—and lost. "We're not running off. We're going independently north for business reasons."

"Mmm." Louise looked off toward the humpies in the distance. "That David. A friend."

"Yes. Maggie's a friend, too. Known her for years."

"Look. Do your friend a favor, huh? Tell him I want his little dog."

"He knows that."

"And tell him I always get what I want sooner or later."

"I doubt that's altogether true."

Louise was looking at her in the darkness with the strangest expression. It seemed a mix of contempt and fear. What had Polly just said to change the girl's expression like that?

Louise smirked. "Then if you know that, I bet you also know that if I can't have it, no one else gets it either. Right-o, mate?"

Polly stood up and retrieved her bucket. "I still didn't fetch the water. I'd best get moving. Nice talking to you," she lied.

"G'night, Polly."

When Polly had walked off, and darkness had blotted Louise away, the girl was still gazing skyward.

Polly scooped a bucketful of water and ambled back to the fire, in no hurry. Out on the track she heard the cranky hum of a motor. A speck of white lamplight intruded on the quiet darkness to the south. She had better things to do than watch approaching traffic. She continued to the fire and ladled a bit more water into the bubbling stew.

Colm sat cross-legged across the fire from her. He straightened and looked out to the south. "Happen to see what's coming?"

"Yes. A brilliant white cyclops. Still just a dot in the distance, come to either devour us or count himself in on the stew."

"Cyclops eat kangaroos?"

"If they eat here, they do. Is it repairable?" She twisted her head aside for a better look at the harness in Colm's lap.

"Nothing baling wire can't fix. Australia's tied together with baling wire." He bent over his work again, pliers in one hand and harness in the other.

"I'd like to see you fix a leaky petrol tank with baling wire. There are advantages to horses you keep forgetting."

He smiled briefly, noncommittally.

"You're no fun to rag." Polly gave the stew an extra stir, although it didn't need it. "You never rise to the bait. But I'll keep trying. Sooner or later, I'll stumble onto something that gets your goat."

Colm looped a tug around his boot, leaned back and pulled mightily on the nether end. "Harness is in worse shape than Jewel. You might consider ordering a motor car when you get back to Corley."

She was trying to frame a snide reply, and not getting very far, when Louise came wandering over. She was carrying Maggie's puppy around again. Why did that bother Polly so? The little dog was tucked in the crook of Louise's left arm, her right hand absentmindedly scratching the chubby neck.

She plopped down beside Colm. "You haven't eaten yet?"

"Tough kangaroo," he answered.

"Good cuisine takes time," Polly answered.

"I got some biscuits left. I'll fetch 'em over then." Louise's voice dropped a couple notches. "Say, Colm. Do me a real big favor, will you?"

"What's that?"

"Explain to your abo chum that I really need this dog. He's a ripper. Gonna be a first-rate watchdog when he's bigger. And a girl living alone—well, you know. Besides, he's good company. Got a neat little personality."

"Tell David that?"

"Yuh. He says 'No worries' with that silly grin of his. Does that mean he's considering it?"

"Nope."

"Didn't think so. Will you talk to him? Huh?"

"It's not his dog. It's Maggie Minnanong's."

"Oh, come on, mate! Break it down. You know that's a line of—"

Her plaint was drowned out by a mechanical wheeze and backfire and internal-combustion belch. The far distant vehicle had arrived. It pulled in beside the fire with only one of its two front lamps burning.

"A cyclops." Colm half smiled at Polly. "Guard the stew." He laid his work aside and stood up as the driver climbed stiffly out of his truck.

Polly followed Colm and everyone else over to the truck. Correction. It was not one vehicle but two. The cyclops was a hulking gasoline lorry, a normal looking (though one-eyed) front end, pulling a cylindrical tank big enough to carry water for a thousand camels. An open motor car was roped to the truck's back axle. The little horseless carriage looked so slight and fragile behind the massive tanker.

A small boy scrambled out of the truck behind its driver. A man and a woman with a baby in her arms followed him down to solid ground. Mr. Myer introduced everyone around, and the driver presented himself and the family with him.

Polly walked around to the back of the tanker, partly to stand in amazement at how such a bulky thing could propel itself down the road, and partly to take another look at the motor car. No doubt about it, this would be a marvelous way to get about, if it didn't break down—as this one obviously had done. A thick crust of dust totally obscured the car's color. Even its seat was covered. It must have spent many a mile attached behind the tanker. Its back was packed, absolutely filled with crates, chairs, a blanket chest and myriad boxes. She felt motion, a presence beside her.

Colm stood at her shoulder staring in rapt admiration at the dusty little conveyance. "She's a beaut. Tarrant touring car, maybe aught-eight or aught-nine."

"She'd be a lot beauter if the motor ran."

117

"Her owner—that Sidney Leland—was describing the problem. Sounds fixable."

"With baling wire, no doubt."

"Maybe." He walked over to the front end of the car, paused only a moment, wrenched a handle and heaved upward. In a startled little poof of dust the whole bonnet lifted. He folded it back gently and peered into blackness.

"Are you sure you know what you're doing? If the truck driver and the owner don't know how to fix it . . ."

He bent forward, groping in the darkness of the little car's innards. "The driver just bought his truck, his first one, he says. In the cavalry during the war and doesn't know much about mechanics. And the owner admits to knowing even less. Got a light of some kind?"

As she walked back toward the fire, Colm called, "Bring the pliers, too." She gave her stew a quick stir and chose an appropriate brand from the fire. She dug the pliers out from under her pile of abandoned harness. When she returned, the knot of chattering people had moved from truckside to carside. Like ostriches, the driver, the trucker and Colm had all buried their heads under the bonnet.

"Here she is." Colm took the brand from her hand and tilted it over the car's interior. It flared up. "See what I'm talking about there?"

"Yuh," the drivers chorused.

Polly stepped back. Mechanics interested her not in the least. On the other hand she had developed a fairly good eye for diagnosing problems in horses. Perhaps she was not made for mechanized travel. She found herself standing beside the weary Mrs. Leland.

"Polly Chase. Did Mr. Myer say your name is Helen?"

The woman nodded.

"So you're the mother of the motor car here."

She snorted. "I wish we'd never seen the beast, and I've told Sid that more than once. I'll take a good horse

118

and wagon any day over these infernal doovers. This is the third time since Daylesford we've broken down. And twice before that."

"Don't know what men see in them." Polly watched the three headless bodies hovering over the car's innards. Normally so stoic, Colm flapped about in an animated explanation of some mysterious process. The car's owner held the torch now. His head bobbed up and down enthusiastically. The truck driver stretched to tiptoe. With the flair of an orchestra conductor, he waved a hand across the whole mechanism.

And now here was Louise, that poor puppy still on her arm. She hopped up on the front bumper and peered in. The mechanics stood up and stepped back. Colm closed the bonnet. The knot of people melted and rearranged itself to accommodate the mechanics.

Polly walked over to Colm. "I suppose our stew is a victim of the cyclops."

"That all right?"

"Sure. Tell them dinner is served." Polly walked off to the fire.

On the way she glanced back and was relieved to see Louise hanging, not on Colm's arm, but on the Lelands'. How could Colm—wise, sensible, insightful Colm—fail to see what the spoiled little brat was doing. *If I don't get it nobody else does, either,* indeed!

On the other hand, unattached women were few and far between in the outback. Every woman in this camp save Louise was married, and that was probably pretty much the ratio everywhere in the bush.

The truck driver arrived at the stewpot almost immediately, greasy hands and all, but the Lelands were elsewhere. Colm hunkered down beside the fire.

Polly handed him a dish of stew also. "Did you invite the Lelands?"

"They're coming. Over with Louise."

"Good. There may be biscuits with this soon, Mr.— did Mr. Myer say Uberholtz?"

"Ya, Uberholtz." The way Mr. Uberholtz

119

pronounced his name and the way the rest of the world attempted it were two different things. "T'ank you for dis hot dinner. Ferry goot. I vass hoping to get on north tonight. Not too far from de opal fields now, you know. Sell my petrol dere. Goot market. Dey buy effert'ing you got to sell."

Polly looked at Colm and smiled. "Let's hope so."

Here came the Lelands, and there was a new lilt to Helen's step, even a smile on her face. Her mood was completely reversed from that of a few minutes before. Was the thought of a meal so invigorating?

And now here came Louise, just as bouncy. She handed her basket of biscuits, not to Polly but to Colm. "They're buttered already." She plopped down beside him. "So you think you can fix it with baling wire."

"Only wire we have." He passed the basket to Mr. Uberholtz.

"Well, I want to tell you right now how much I appreciate it." Louise was smug as a cat with canary feathers in its fur.

"Oh, you do."

She giggled. "Too right. It's my car."

Polly's head snapped around toward the Lelands. No wonder Mrs. Leland looked so relieved and happy! "You traded the car for Louise's wagon?"

Louise beamed. "Straight across the board. Wanna sell some petrol before you head north, Mr. Uberholtz?"

"De tanks are full. Vhat if you can't get it running?"

Louise shrugged. "I'm in no hurry. I'll just hang around here until someone comes along who can help. Or Colm can send someone down from the opal fields. Must be mechanics there. I think they even have telegraph service. He can send out for parts."

"Dangerous, sitting out here alone." Colm gave her biscuit basket back to her.

She smiled knowingly. "I'm armed. No worries." She said it with that same carefree inflection David used. "Course, what I really need's a dog."

Colm set his bowl aside. "Let me work on it a little now. Maybe we can get it perking before Mr. Uberholtz leaves. It'll be better if you can convoy out with him. Sid? Myer? Might I borrow your help?" He dug the baling wire out of the pile of harness.

With Louise tagging along, the three men trotted off to one of man's few projects that might take precedence over eating. Polly finished her stew in silence, only half listening as Mrs. Leland and Mrs. Pitts jabbered like village farm wives at the back fence. She could scarce contain her own pleasure. With a car that goes fifteen miles an hour—or more—Louise could not in any way stay with this party that averaged only fifteen miles a day. She might fall behind or jackrabbit ahead, but she would no longer be purring and cooing at Colm.

—until Coober Pedy.

What then? Polly would address that problem when she reached it. But then, why was it a problem at all? She was a married woman with no interest in Colm other than a business arrangement, a share in his fortunes as an opal miner. Harmless friendship and a grubstake—that was all. If Colm and Louise pursued each other, what was that to her? Louise was unusual, evensay dark and ominous at times. She tended to think quite a bit of herself. But no one's perfect, and a hearty dollop of self-confidence helps a great deal out here in the bush. She was Colm's problem, if at all, not Polly's. Polly kept telling herself that, but she could not bring herself to believe it.

A motor coughed and gurgled.

"Ha!" Mr. Uberholtz grinned. "Listen to dat! He's a miracle verker, dat Stawell fellow."

"Isn't he! Why, hello, David! There's still some stew left. Not much, but enough to keep you going another four or five hours at least. Where are your friends?"

David materialized fully from the darkness on the edge of the campfire glow. He plunked down in the spot Colm had vacated and waved an arm. "That way

121

three, four miles. They think they'll go down to Ood-nadatta. I been there too soon. Go up Larrapinta more."

Polly wagged her head. "So you take off across the wastes all alone and don't think twice about it."

David's eyes and teeth twinkled in the firelight. "Too right. All alike, here, there. Take Maggie's dog to her. Watch her face."

Mr. Uberholtz wiggled a finger at David. "Tell me, ya? Iss true you knock out your tooth vhen you become a man?"

"Don't hafta. Best ones do."

"So that's why the gap. I didn't know." Polly handed him the last of the stew and a spoon. "How? Who? I'm not sure how to phrase the question politely."

David mimed the motions. "Take a sharp stick. Hold it here." He pointed to his gap. "Rock for a hammer. Whack! All done."

Polly shuddered.

Louise came bouncing over to the fire and settled near David. "David dear cobber, we've a deal to strike here."

Suddenly, unexpectedly, David grabbed the pup from Louise's arm. He whistled. Here came the momma dog. David plopped the puppy down near her and the two both bounded off beyond the fire ring. He went back to his stew. "Not mine."

"Then pass the proceeds on to the owner. That Maggie." Louise laid a ten-pound note on his bare knee. "David, I really like that old bitzer, right-o? I need him. Maggie can get any old dog. There's a million around blackfellers' camps, but none around white-fellers' camps."

"Spoke for. Sorry." David gave her a cheery, boyish grin.

Louise glared at him a long, long moment. What did David see? He made no sign that he saw anything. And yet Aborigines are extremely sensitive, extremely good at reading emotion in others. He must have perceived

122

the pure, intense anger in her eyes. She burned with something far more intense than anger. Even Polly could see that. Strange girl. Dark.

Louise leaped up suddenly and jogged off toward her wagon. Polly really ought to go help the Lelands unload that horrendous pile of belongings from the touring car. She ought to help Louise load up, although Louise did not seem to own much in the way of transferable possessions. But both Pittses were on their feet and headed that way, and there went Mr. Hargreaves. Louise had help enough.

Polly watched David awhile. He engulfed his stew as if he feared it was poised to flee his bowl. He waved his spoon at her and spoke with his mouth full. "Next time, younger kangaroo, right-o?"

The car's rough motor died with a grateful sigh. Shortly Colm entered the ring of firelight and hunkered down next to David. He scooped up his bowl and with a happy smile rattled something off. David laughed and rattled something else right back.

Mr. Uberholtz stood up. "Shall I vash the dish out somevhere?"

"No, don't bother. That's fine." Polly smiled at him.

"Ah, vell. I t'ank you immensely for de meal. Can I pay?"

"Of course not. The kangaroo was free. And if you saw the condition the potatoes were in, we would've had to pay you."

He chuckled. "Vass a pleasure. Miss Flett iss coming vit' me, den?"

Colm nodded. "She's getting her stuff out of her wagon. Claims she knows how to drive a car. Probably needs help cranking it."

"Goot night, Missus Chase." Mr. Uberholtz dissolved into the darkness, headed for Louise's wagon. Ex-wagon.

Here came the mother dog. She pressed against David's elbow begging, her tail flopping wildly. Colm passed a bit of potato over to David and David passed it on. The tail went insane. David teased her a moment, then fished a chunk of meat out of his own bowl for her. She licked his fingers. Her puppy climbed over her rump and tumbled into David's lap.

Polly watched David's face, fascinated. The man was leather tough and twice as strong to make his life in this barren country with nothing more than a bowl and a spear. He could travel faster and farther than a man on horseback. He could probably outfight any man Polly had ever met, including Colm. Yet here he sat childlike, totally delighted, totally gentle, in intimate camaraderie with two dogs. Colm, too, was that sort of man. No wonder they were such fast friends. David scraped the last spoonful into his mouth and held his bowl for the dogs to lick clean.

Polly turned her attention to Colm. "Jealous?" she asked presently.

"Of a couple of dogs?"

"Of a slip of a girl who now owns your dream machine."

"Leland got the best of it."

"Oh my! Sour grapes, too."

The truck motor grunted and roared. The cyclopian eye flared to life.

Louise took shape in the firelight. She was back in trousers again and she had tucked some sort of medium-sized pistol in her rope belt. She wasn't lying when she said she was armed. Didn't she trust the soft-spoken Mr. Uberholtz? Or did she always have that gun somewhere close at hand in her wagon? Polly guessed the latter.

Louise looked at Colm. "I'm on my way. Thanks again for getting that thing to run, and for showing me how to keep it going."

"Happy to." Colm finished off the last of his supper; it must be cold by now.

"G'bye, Polly. See you up north."

"Yes." Polly nodded to her. "Goodbye."

Colm stood up suddenly and extended his hand. "God bless you with a safe journey."

"Thank you." She took his hand, but only as a lever to pull him in close enough for a goodbye kiss. It wasn't on the cheek, either. Polly was shocked speechless. She felt her mouth drop open. Of all the brazen, blatant—

Louise turned to David. "I won't take no for an answer. Name your price." Her voice had that hard edge again. Were she a man with a deeper voice, Polly would have dived for cover.

There was no smile now. David's iron core had surfaced. "No, mum."

"It's only a dog, hang you! A worthless mutt that's going to grow up into a cur like these others. It's not even half grown. I'm offering you a thousand times what it's worth. Stop being stupid!"

"Louise," Colm purred, "it's not his."

Her voice was building. "I need a dog. I need that dog, train it up for what I want. *I* deserve that dog, not some dirty abo." She started toward David, but Colm's long arm stopped her.

"Did you tell him what I said?" Louise was turning on Polly now.

Polly said nothing. How do you reason with a person who has obviously just tipped her cookies off the shelf?

She glared at Colm's impassive face, then at David. "Animals don't keep animals. Tell 'em, Polly. Tell 'em what's good for 'em."

"Maggie's my friend, Louise. I said that."

"And nobody's *my* friend, right?" She twisted aside, throwing off Colm's arm. "Give me my dog!" Near hysteria, her voice and hands shook.

From the darkness beyond came Mr. Uberholtz's voice, ending in a question mark.

David studied the fire and scratched the mother dog absently behind the ears. Her puppy fell off his lap and waddled away toward Polly's bowl.

"No stinking abo's gonna have my dog!" Like metal, Louise's voice sheared through the heavy darkness.

Everything registered at once, so quickly Polly could not move. Louise flailed wildly; the pistol in her hand exploded; the puppy skipped two feet across the dirt with one piercing yelp.

Colm grabbed Louise's wrist. The pistol fired again skyward. With his other hand he wrenched the gun away from her and flung it off into the darkness. He grasped her in two mighty handfuls and shook her as one might shake an errant child.

"David!" he roared. "You almost hit David!" He gave her a hard shove away from himself, emptying his hands of her.

She staggered backward two stumbling steps and fell hard on her bottom. Cat-quick, she rolled to her feet. She paused the barest moment to look from face to face, her own features disfigured by rage. She wheeled and ran into the blackness toward the rumbling truck.

It was over. Those gunshots and Colm's thundering voice reduced the engine noises to deep and brooding silence. Polly's hands shook too hard to do anything save press themselves against her cheeks. People were standing around gaping, as dumbstruck as she.

Another engine fired up and two headlights wiped out another piece of the smothering darkness. The motors and the lights lumbered, waddling, out onto the track. Their sounds and their glow faded into the night.

Colm stared at Polly, uncomprehending, and Polly stared back just as uncomprehending. What personal demons so possessed Louise that she would do this? What dark shadows drove her hands and bent her mind?

The mother dog was whimpering. With an audible sigh, David picked up the limp, bloody little fur-ball.

His voice was velvet soft with sadness. "I'll tell Maggie what happened. But never—I can never tell her *why*."

126

CHAPTER 12

SO MUCH OF AUSTRALIA'S scenery can be drawn
with a ruler. To the west of the track, the horizon
stretched dead level to eternity. To the east rose another of those sets of low ridges so fondly overrated
by the Aussies. Polly rather preferred the low hills to
California's steep mountains; they were much, much
easier to traverse.

The winter's grass had not quite all dried up. Here
and there a few tinges of pallid green remained. Most
of the soil was pale pinkish peach and barren.

They were passing now another patch of patty melons. Dying vines sprawled all over the ground. Dozens
of chartreuse melons, some the size of undernourished
tennis balls and others over eight inches long, lay hap-
hazardly about.

Polly pointed. "Ever taste one of those?"

Colm nodded. "I'll eat the soles of my boots first.
Burning rubber smells better than those things taste.
They aren't native, you know."

"They're all over along the roadside."

"I hear the camel drivers would scatter the seed as

127

they passed. They wanted a constant supply of fodder for their camels, and camels eat the melons."

"Really. I thought a camel would have better taste. It's not the most intelligent looking beast in the world, of course. But patty melons?"

"Cattle won't touch 'em. Neither will kangaroos, and you can't get much dimmer than a 'roo."

Polly watched with renewed interest another passing patch. She giggled. "An Afghani Johnny Appleseed."

"Johnny Appleseed?"

"Well! I finally touched upon something you never heard about." Polly was about to regale him with all the legends she could remember about the American folk hero when she saw a little white cone of dirt sitting on the pink flats. She frowned and pointed.

Colm pointed beyond her ear toward the ridges. "Couple more back there. See 'em?"

"Can't be termites."

"Opal mines."

"Oh, come! They're so—so nondescript. Just a little pile of sand."

"This one," he pointed out, "is pretty small. And you see nothing's been added to it for a long while. Some miner dug around a little, decided it wasn't promising enough and abandoned it."

She twisted in her seat to watch it a moment longer. "So ordinary. I can't believe something as gorgeous as that opal could come out of a nondescript pile of dirt."

"Know how sometimes a hill or ridge will be built up in layers? Stripes? The land beneath us is like that. Layers eight or ten feet thick, one on top of the other. Hargreaves explained it to me. The opals form as nodules between layers. You pick yourself a likely spot and drop a hole straight down, until the line between two layers is about eye level. Then you start digging sideways. If the Lord smiles on you, you find opals here and there between the layers. If He doesn't, you dig for nothing or go down another level."

"How do you know where to stake your claim? Where to start?"

"That's the trick."

"It's an awful lot of dirt to move for a few handfuls of opal. Or is it solid rock?"

"Sandstone, I think. But soft. Chisel it. Mild explosives."

"Mmm. I heard Mr. Hargreaves boasting about his skill with explosives. You be careful around them. Around him, too. I don't care how skilled he thinks he is."

"Yes, mother."

Polly's cheeks flushed. "You know what I mean. He was saying how Ballarat miners are the best explosives experts in the world, and I never trust a boastful person."

"He's right. Ballarat miners have a reputation for getting the most work out of the least amount of powder."

A rickety truck came chugging along the road toward them. Colm moved Jewel off to the left of the track and watched with unabashed admiration as the dirty little box on wheels grumbled past. "Chain drive, probably about ten years old."

"They all look alike to me." Polly thought of the attraction Louise's touring car must have on Colm and shuddered. Perhaps part of the charm of these noisy, peevish, petrol-drinking monsters was the very fact that they did indeed break down, and that Colm most often could put them back to rights. Each miraculous repair job was another little triumph of the spirit. She used to think her father a bit strange, but then professors are supposed to be. She considered Peter difficult to fathom sometimes. But Colm was worse than either of them. All men must be a puzzle.

The cream-colored cones were more frequent now, and taller. Wooden trestles like poppetheads stuck out of some of them.

"Up ahead," Polly pointed. "Some buildings there."

Colm craned his neck to see beyond Myers's wagon and twisted to call back to Hargreaves.

Hargreaves grinned. "Looks so, mate. I think we're there."

Polly stared. "That's Coober Pedy? There's nothing there!"

"Remember what David was saying? A lot of it's underground—out of sight."

"But—" Polly closed her mouth.

The place had a couple buildings, most of them slapped together of gray planks or corrugated tin. Narrow little sheds lined dusty, unpaved streets. Perhaps the sheds were the entranceways into more spacious underground quarters. Now here was quite a basic arrangement: The tip of a crude wooden ladder disappeared down a simple round hole by the road. Alice in Wonderland.

Trucks and horse wagons were parked all around here and there. Polly looked for the touring car and did not see it. Horses apparently lived aboveground. Polly saw sheds and corrals all over the place also.

Colm drew Jewel aside and the Pitts wagon swung out around, to continue on. "There's a barber shop. You inquire there and I'll go find an accommodation."

"My home-grown haircuts aren't good enough for you anymore."

He hopped to the ground and gave her a gentlemanly hand down. "Bartenders, barbers, and postmasters know everything about everyone. The barber can tell you how to go about selling your lace and whether there's telegraph service. Ask him about the best place to eat. I'll put Jewel up, get us each a room and meet you here. We'll compare notes on the best eating place."

"Sounds efficient." She stepped down into the dust and rejoiced in the feel of solid ground beneath her feet. "I won't ask whether you're inquiring at the bar or the post office." She scratched Jewel's chin a moment as she passed around the front. Then her wagon went rattling off down the street without her.

She completed her business with the barber in fifteen minutes. It would have been five minutes were he not so talkative. Colm was right, though; he was such a gold mine of information that she now knew where the post office and major stores were, not to mention the best restaurant in Australia. She looked up and down the track—she could hardly call it a street when there were so few buildings of any sort. You could not even tell where the street ended and the sideways began. Colm was nowhere in sight.

She walked to the post office and rented a box. She introduced herself to the postmaster and to his assistant. When she walked back out, Colm was still not to be seen. There was much to be said for such an open town; you could see everyone just about anywhere.

She descended into a dry goods store the barber had recommended. An absolutely cavernous room had been carved from living rock. Thick stone columns supported the ceiling here and there. The store was almost as nicely stocked as was Wiggins's, but they offered their customers very little lace. What they had was machine-made and of inferior quality.

Triumphantly she whipped her samples from her handbag.

When she jogged up the store's steps ten minutes later, she saw Colm's tall form near the post office. He was leaning on the fender of a touring car talking to the slight, auburn-haired driver! The little fox must not have wasted a minute bailing him up.

Colm turned toward her as she came hurrying up to them.

"Eh, Polly! Hullo!" Louise was all charming smiles, as if she had not recently committed an atrocity.

"Hello." Polly made certain her voice was cold enough to freeze the water in Louise's radiator.

Colm nodded toward the touring car owner. "Louise says she'd like to take us to the world's finest restaurant."

131

"The world's finest restaurant is in San Francisco."
Polly built a false smile and stuck it out front where
Louise could see it. "Perhaps some other time. Thank
you."

Colm looked at her steadily with question marks in
his smoky eyes. Polly felt no need to answer.

He stood erect suddenly and nodded toward Louise.
"Take you up on it another day, aye? Thank you."

"Right-o." The crocodile smile never left Louise's
face. "We'll be bumping into each other. Good to see
you made it here fine. Hooroo."

"Hooroo." Polly let her own hypocritical smile fade.

Colm gave the touring car's crank a turn and Louise
was on her way. He watched the car manufacture a
dust cloud. "We're called upon by our Lord to forgive."

"I'm sorry. I can't. Is there a hotel here?"

He dug into his pocket, nodding. "You're room four.
Mine's fifteen, out back in a courtyard. Jewel's munching hay in the yard behind the hotel. The best restaurant in Australia is Barney's over by the chapel." He
gave her a key.

"The barber mentioned Barney's, too. And there's
a place that specializes in yard-fed beef, over beyond
the dry goods store. Colm, this place is creepy in a
way. Ominous."

"Just a matter of getting used to it. Hungry?"

"Very. Let's go. I can hardly wait to eat something
that doesn't taste like a kangaroo." She fell in beside
him and was hard-pressed to keep up with his long,
swinging strides. He must be hungry, too.

"Checked around any about selling lace?"

"Better than that. The dry goods merchant already
says he'll take whatever I can provide him. He was
just delighted. And he offered me five times what I was
offered in Corley. I have to look around a couple other
places yet, but it seems I can sell as much as I can
make. I hate to admit it, but you're a financial genius."

"Genius. Without a brass razoo to my name."

"A temporary condition, I'm certain. Oh, and I rented

a postal box. One-thirty-three. It's in my name; I didn't want some dim government employee making a mistake and holding back a letter from Peter or the army. Two keys," she dug them out of her handbag. "One for you and one for me. You're welcome to take it over completely when I leave."

When I leave. Were she driving a motor car, her radiator, too, would have been frozen solid by those icy words. She regretted saying them instantly.

Colm seemed not to notice. "And the bartender told me about a fellow over among the buttes who's looking to sell his claim. It might pay me to go talk to him. He's got a shaft down and an operation in full swing. Save me a lot of time."

"Would he want to sell if he were actually finding any opals?"

"Bartender seems to think he's one of those people who finds manual labor not worth the effort. You have to put twelve hours a day into your mine, and he's not quite up to donating six. This must be Barney's. Wait a moment, aye?"

The entrance to the restaurant and the chapel entrance both butted into the side of a steep pink hillside. Polly waited by Barney's galvanized tin shed. Colm walked over to the chapel and studied a little sign by the door.

He came strolling back, smiling. "Thought they might have the times posted for worship services. They do."

He opened Barney's door for her. They walked down half a dozen steps and along a dark passageway into another of those cavernous rooms. This one was furnished, not with dry goods, but with tables and chairs and checkered tablecloths.

"I can't believe it. Eating like real human beings. No dirt to fall in the food."

He smirked. "Feel the walls."

She reached out with her fingertips. The cavern walls still bore the marks of drills and pick-axes. The wall surface was crumbly, almost sandy. "It's still not the same. I'm sure it's much more difficult here to kick dead grass and stones into your kidney pie."

Colm seated her at a table to one side. She looked around at the lights, as bright and modern as those in any big city, and the flat hard stone floor. A ventilation shaft went up through the ceiling and no doubt there were more than just that one. She looked at the elaborate lamps attached to the bulky ceiling support columns.

"What happens when the electricity fails?"

"I hear you haven't seen darkness until the lights go out in here."

Another of those little chills danced up her spine. "Colm, I have the strangest feeling about this place. Not just the restaurant here or any one building, or hole, if you will. The whole place. Please do be careful about explosives and that sort of thing. Will you?"

She expected another retort.

Instead he was locking into her eyes with his own, and they were sad eyes. "I'm safe, Polly. Satan can't touch me. Death can't touch me. It's you I'm worried about."

"Colm, that's silly." But it wasn't silly. She knew it as soon as she said it. It wasn't silly at all.

"If I die right now, I stand before the risen Christ. He promised, and I accepted His promise. But you haven't yet, you know. You've never acknowledged that Jesus is alive and that He's the only one worthy of being your Master."

"Well, uh, everyone knows that." She tried to look away and could not. "I'm not really that big on theology, as you know. Not like you and Peter. I can discuss the literary merits of the Bible for hours, but religion, as such—" She shrugged. Where was a waiter when you needed one? She wanted an interruption.

"Have you ever done anything you'd consider wrong?"

"Well, certainly. Everyone has, I suspect."

"Too right. And do you want God to hold it against you, or do you want Him to forgive you?"

"Forgive me, of course, with a choice like that. But no. 'Forgive us our debts as we forgive our debtors.' Colm, I can't forgive Louise. I never could. She's insane. I'm certain of it. Something tips her off the edge and she goes berserk. She's dangerous."

"We're not talking about Louise. We're talking about you. Tonight read the Book of Romans for me. Will you, please? The whole book."

"If you like," she murmured, and here came the waiter.

Peter, Colm is getting even more fanatical than you are! Make contact quickly, please! Suddenly I feel very uncomfortable here.

CHAPTER 13

PAULETTE BELINDA UPSHAW CHASE HAD earned a *cum laude* degree in literature. Even on that little farm beyond Corley Bore, she had maintained her skills and interest in good reading. Her subscription to the *Bulletin* still had half a year on it. She should be able to take any well-written piece in the English language and extract the essence of it, right? Everyone agreed the Bible was well written. So why could not college graduate Polly Chase see in this simple piece of literature whatever it was that Colm Stawell with no degree whatever thought she ought to see?

She stared at her Bible on the nightstand beside the bed. She was grateful the hotel here was built aboveground. The morning sun streamed in and helped brighten her mood. Flopping onto the bed, she propped herself to sitting with the pillow and scooped the Bible into her lap. She had read the Book of Romans last night as requested, but no lightning had struck. What was the mystery here?

Colm wanted her to see something. He was in tune with God. Therefore it was safe to assume that God, too, wanted her to see something. Colm was out among the ridges this morning talking to that fellow, but God was here. Perhaps Polly should ask God to help her see what Colm wanted her to.

She laughed aloud. Polly Chase, *cum laude* grad, was asking a God she did not really know to help her interpret literature! Unimaginable. And yet it seemed also quite sensible. This was Colm's doing; somehow he had changed her thinking to the point where she accepted God as Colm accepted Him—a Person willing to help out now and then.

Very well. She asked God specifically to make Himself known and to guide her reading of the Word. And she meant it; she assured Him of that. She broke the Bible open to Romans and began again.

Chapter one: Paul's greeting and preliminary.

Chapter two: She did not fit any of that list of sins at the end, except maybe foolishness and disobedience to parents.

Chapter three: "None is righteous." She knew that, having heard it from both Peter and Colm.

Chapter four: God's promises are valid for anyone who has faith. That certainly included Peter and Colm.

Chapter five: Everyone has sinned but only one Person cancelled all that sin—Jesus.

Chapter six: The last verse gripped her attention like an iron fist. "The wages of sin is death; but the gift of God is eternal life through Jesus Christ our Lord." How often she had heard that! Colm was certain he could not die. He was certain she would. He was sure he had the gift and she did not. Yet never was he the least bit haughty about it; never did his manner suggest "I'm better than you." She recalled again the sadness in his eyes.

Chapter seven: All that convoluted stuff, once she ironed it out, fit her perfectly. It was Polly! The things she wanted to do didn't get done. The things she knew she shouldn't do seemed to happen anyway. Paul said he didn't understand his own actions. Well, Polly didn't understand hers either. She constantly talked a good line in her mind and never followed through in real life. Who delivered that wretched man Paul? Jesus Christ! Who therefore could deliver Polly? The same, Jesus!

Chapter eight: The first verse was all she needed. *There is therefore now no condemnation to those which are in Christ Jesus.* She closed the Book.

She was traveling a path now which she knew Colm had already followed over a year ago, and which Peter had followed years before them. It was the same path, although every man and woman entered, it seemed, by a different way. And yet, perhaps not. Polly, with all her fancy literature skills, had to ask for divine help before the path became clear to her.

Never in her life had Polly ever prayed on her knees. She scooted off the bed to do that now. She asked God to forgive her and seal her into the mastery and service of Jesus Christ. When several minutes later she finally stood up, she didn't really expect any lightning flash. She was not a lightning-flash sort of person. She did fully expect God to reveal Himself—to show her His reality—in some way He would choose, some way that would mean something not to Colm or to Peter or even to the apostle Paul, but to Polly. She trusted God completely to do that; was this faith?

Suddenly that bright morning sunshine flickered like a candle when compared to the brightness she felt inside. Her mouth spread into a grin she could not suppress, not that she wanted to. She could feel it! She was a sister to Colm Stawell, and she could not wait until he got back, that she might tell him so.

She ought to put the morning to use, however. She could not simply sit about, basking in her inner sunshine. She unpacked her boxes of lace and chose about a third of her complete stock to take to the dry goods merchant. If he wanted more, she would provide it.

Still floating on clouds, she bounced out into the sunshine and morning heat. The barren ground reflected brightness upon her from all directions. She glowed from inside out and from outside in.

Business at the dry goods store didn't take long at all. The proprietor examined nearly every inch of her lace and seemed much pleased by its quality. She left the store with a draft so large she walked in a daze.

The bank was next, of course. She established an account simply to have somewhere to keep her money safe until she left. At two percent per year, she did not expect too much of a bonanza in interest.

Where was Colm? She so wanted to tell him! There was Mrs. Pitts. Polly walked over and chatted a few minutes, saying nothing, watching for Colm. Mrs. Pitts went on about her business and Polly went on about her own. Actually, she had no pressing business, but she might as well stop by the post office. The luxury of being able to check for mail more than once a month was just too fine to resist.

She fumbled her key and opened box one-thirty-three. Look at that! Less than twenty-four hours a patron, already she had two pieces of mail. One was Peter's paycheck, detained less than three weeks by the forwarding process. Her heart thudded to a halt. The other was also from the war department, a Major General in Melbourne. The envelope was not quite the same color as the paycheck envelope, nor was it from specifically the same cubbyhole in the vast army labyrinth. After all these months of awaiting an answer, Polly could not bear to open it. She stepped out into the sun-brilliance.

How silly! Of course she must open it. Peter was still in Europe or he was serving in Palestine or he was on his way home now. Just barely possibly, but certainly not probably, this end of the labyrinth would tell her he was dead and the other end, the paycheck end, had never gotten the word. No. As Colm said, the army's a frugal sport.

But waiting was over at last. At least now she would know. She took a deep deep breath—and another for good measure—and opened the Major General's letter.

She read it once through quickly and puzzled at how

the army could have confused Peter's records with someone else's. Obviously something had gotten all at crossed tracks. Perhaps she'd best travel to Melbourne and try to straighten this out in person. She would wire Corley first, of course, and make certain Peter was not waiting for her there.

She read it again with difficulty. Her eyes, overflowing and flooding down her cheeks, could not see the print well.

This letter is written in response to your enquiry regarding the whereabouts of your husband Chaplain Peter Murchison Chase 354-6777-8929CCQ. We wish to inform you that Chaplain Chase is a patient in the Army Veterans Hospital, 18th Street and Burwood Way, Melbourne. According to military record, Chaplain Chase was wounded in the line of duty 5 June 1915. After several months' recuperation at facilities in and near the Mediterranean theatre, he arrived in Melbourne via steamship *Pamphylia* 18 November 1915. He has been housed at the veterans hospital above from 20 November 1915 to the present.

Hospital records indicate that Chaplain Chase suffered severe brain injury the direct result of his war wound and that the damage is apparently irreversible. His condition has failed to respond well to rehabilitation efforts. Although he is capable of standing briefly if supported, and will eat if hand-fed, he does not seem to recognize faces, nor does he respond to the human voice or to most external stimuli. He is not in control of most bodily functions.

We regret that the news concerning your husband could not be better and we are dismayed that our notification to you of his arrival in Australia failed to reach you. If we may be of further service, kindly write using the correspondence file number shown below.

Where was Colm? He could explain this. She stumbled and almost bumped into a passing miner. She must return to the hotel, to Colm's room. He would know.

Dear God, I was prepared for his return and I was prepared for his death. I was not prepared for this!

She slammed in through the front door of the hotel before she realized she had arrived at this end of town. She ran out into the courtyard behind and to room fifteen. She pounded on the door.

Colm swung the door open agonizing moments later. "G'day, mum. Lunchtime. I was about to see if—" His voice dribbled away. His face was wet, his sleeves rolled up, and he was holding a towel. He stared at her. He looked at the letters in her hand.

Unable to speak, she handed them to him and stepped inside. He closed the door and gave Peter's paycheck back to her. He wandered off across the room as he slipped the Major General's letter from its envelope.

His face, normally impassive, twisted. The mouth drew in tight. He wheeled suddenly to face her and his eyes were on fire.

"It's not fair!" The thundering voice of this massive man who filled the room sounded on the verge of tears. Wildly he flung his towel against the wall. "All those nights I lay up in that cold barn loft, praying that if for any reason Peter didn't take you, that I could have you. I begged God! How could He do this?"

"Colm—" Her knees were getting rubbery. She groped for a chair.

His left hand began opening and closing, methodically crunching the letter up smaller and smaller until it was a hard little wad buried in his fist. He waved the fist toward Polly. "Now He does this to me! To you! To Peter! Peter can't have you and I can't have you and you can't—" He sucked in air, more a sob than a gasp.

He was trying to control his rage; she could read it in his face.

"Why!!" he exploded. He flung the wad as violently as he had flung the towel. The bit of paper whacked solidly against the wall.

"Colm?" Her lips trembled; she could barely speak. "Do you realize what you're saying?"

141

"Yes! Yes, I know what I'm saying! I'm saying I love you. I've loved you for months—ever since you let me drain your water can on the road to Corley. It took me awhile to figure out and another while to admit it to myself, but that's what happened. I was in love with a married woman. And I kept hoping the marriage wasn't quite the final thing a marriage ought to be. Maybe he was dead, or he'd found someone or—now this."

He spent a few moments simply breathing, taking in air from deep down. His voice dropped a notch. "Oh the battles I fought. What's lust and what's no more than the appreciation of a good friend? Where does friendship end and sin begin?" He turned to face her. "I asked you to come with me because I couldn't bear to leave you behind. Even if I couldn't have it all, I had to be near you as long as possible. It was better than nothing." The voice softened to a sad rumble. "I suppose I was waiting for some kind of a miracle. A fairy-tale ending." He stared across the room at the wad of paper. "Shoulda known the army doesn't believe in fairy tales."

Polly closed her weary, burning eyes. Her last hope had been that the letter was somehow wrong; that when the army said *this* it really meant *that* instead. That hope was dead, along with all her other hopes and dreams. She was now married to a vegetable.

Colm sagged drunkenly against the far wall, his strength spent. He rubbed the back of his neck, and his face was still wet from the washbowl. "Know what you're going to do yet?"

"Not yet."

He pushed away from the wall presently and slogged across the room like a zombie. He retrieved her letter and tried ineffectually to smooth it out again. "Sorry," he muttered as he handed it to her.

"No worries. I'll just iron it. I'm not really interested in lunch. Dinner perhaps?"

He nodded. "I'll stop by your room around seven."

She nodded, too, and stood up. He held the door for her and she examined the rough floor closely as she left. She strolled across the courtyard in no hurry and returned to her room. There on the bedside table was her Bible. She had forgotten to tell Colm about her joy in Jesus.

Joy. She plopped down on her bed. Joy. Almost numbly she dragged the Bible across the bedspread to her, rolled on her side and opened it to Romans eight, where she had left off those centuries ago this morning.

Yes, centuries it was since she read that first verse. There might be no condemnation, but there wasn't much joy, either. Her eyes followed from line to line registering the words, but her brain was not repeating the registry.

Romans 8:28. Her eyes stopped. She read it three times, and every time it came out the same. *And we know that all things work together for good to them that love God, to them who are the called according to his purpose.*

No, we do not know that, Paul. She could not begin to believe this verse, not in the face of the blow she had just received. She closed the book again and dropped over to her back.

The ceiling plaster was cracked in long dark lines, like the maps of rivers.

Know what you're going to do yet? Colm assumed she had some choices. What choices did she have exactly? She had married Peter for better or for worse and this was definitely worse. On the other hand, he recognized nobody and that would include her. Vegetables don't realize they're married; they don't even know what it means. If she never saw him again, he would never know or care. She could have the marriage dissolved without difficulty. No one would bind her in marriage to a man with irreversible brain damage.

Colm had professed his love for her, and now that she could freely examine her own heart, she could see that she loved him, too. At last she could admit it to herself. Peter did not love her. Peter did not love. Period. He was a book closed, a chapter finished, just as college had been and the quake had been and her childhood had been.

A lifetime with Colm! She still owned the farm and he was happy there. They could try opal mining until the lease ran out and then decide whether to continue as miners or return to being farmers. They could have a wonderful life together!

And Peter would sit in the veterans hospital. And sit. And sit.

Was he really as insensate as the letter indicated? Would he respond to the woman he had once loved so ardently? Clearly he was ruined, for such damage never fully repairs itself. That fine, sharp mind was a shambles, the clever wit dulled, the non-stop verbalization at last silenced. He was no longer the Peter Chase she had married. But he was still Peter Chase.

For hours she tussled with herself. Her decision now would not affect her own happiness only, but Colm's, for years to come. Perhaps even Peter's. She cried almost non-stop. But by late afternoon she had made her decision.

Colm Stawell loved her and his God so much that he had kept his distance all these months. He had kept himself pure; he had kept pure the woman he loved. He had kept pure her commitment to a man he had never met.

But love is only part of a marriage. There is also the responsibility to a promise made at its beginning. She had promised not just to Peter but before God. Oh, true, she did not know God then, not the way she did now. But nonetheless she had promised in His presence to remain true to Peter. She could do nothing less than keep that promise. To abandon Peter would be to soil her commitment to Peter and at the same time spoil the beginning of any new relationship with Colm.

In short, God had accepted her promise to stay with

Peter for better or for worse, in sickness and in health. She would honor her promise.

And then the tears began in earnest—tears for her shattered dreams, for Peter's shattered body, for Colm's shattered love; tears for the gross unfairness of life itself.

The tears had just barely ended when Colm came knocking on her door at seven.

Oh Peter, I'm so sorry it's this way. But I'm yours and you're mine, and we'll both just have to make the best of it.

CHAPTER 14

CROWS DON'T LIKE MOTOR CARS. A cloud of black—
scores of crows—came bursting noisily out of a little
grove of mulgas as the vehicle chugged by. Wedge-
tailed eagles don't like motor cars. Two of the huge,
nondescript brown scavengers lifted off some luckless
carcass a hundred yards south and flapped away casually on easy wings.

Frankly, Polly didn't like motor cars all that much
either, but she certainly preferred riding in this machine, noisy and dusty as it was, to bouncing along in
a wagon at Jewel's pace. She glanced over at Colm on
her right. He sat smugly in the driver's side of an open
touring car, and he was savoring every precious moment of it.

Actually, it was not motor cars Polly disliked; it was
only this one, for this was Louise's Tarrant. Louise
had insisted almost violently that Colm use it. Colm
and Polly had consented mostly to avoid a scene with
the dark strange girl. Of course Louise would be glad
Polly was going to Melbourne; the sooner, the better.
She wasn't offering the car out of some sense of neigh-
borliness but rather for sheer speed in dumping Polly.

Besides, if Colm fell in love with her car (and already he had), perhaps she might expect some of the affection to rub off onto its owner. Polly could read the snip's motives clearly and she was constantly mystified and disappointed that Colm could not. Or would not.

The country here was fairly level, with minor dips and rises. The road skirted a dank swamp in a low spot, lined about with coolabah trees and all buzzy with flies. Over most of the land saltbush and bunch grass filled the open space between mulga forests. Polly surveyed the sky and found four soaring hawks, not counting those two eagles.

She gestured skyward. "I've never quite gotten used to the huge number of kites and hawks. In America you see them only occasionally. Here you can spot one just about any time you look up, and often there's more than one."

"You have foxes and wolves in America? Wildcats?"

"Not many wolves. Foxes, bobcats, lots of coyotes. Mountain lions. I see what you're saying. Our predators are on the ground, yours are in the sky."

He nodded. "Dingos are our only dogs, and no cats. None of your weasel tribe. I read a book about North American natural history once."

"Is there anything you haven't read a book about?"

"Astronomy. Suppose if your father sends you a package sometime, he might put in an astronomy book?"

"Certainly." The question caught her short. Except for that very first time they met, when he asked for a drink, this was the only time he had voluntarily requested something. She must write to her father immediately.

She had more than just astronomy books to write about. After a very short time in Coober Pedy, here she was traversing the weary, monotonous miles to the railroad stop. Why could God not have buried his opals closer to a good railroad? Better, why could South Australia not have built its main line closer to God's opal deposits? It was a simple matter of men not being in tune with God. And wasn't that the problem with the whole world!

Soon she would board the southbound train. The rail gauge changed at the border, so she would have to switch trains to continue down through New South Wales and Victoria—an instance this time of man not being in tune with man. Still she would reach Melbourne within a week or two, a much much shorter journey than that interminable trek from Corley to Coober Pedy.

She had already written to her mother about the army's letter. But what else could she say? She would know nothing certain until she had come to Peter himself. She did not mention Colm specifically, though she did tell her mother about her new relationship with God.

Just exactly what was her new relationship to God? Would she ever feel as comfortable, as free and easy, with God as Colm and Peter did—well, used to? She hoped so. And as she read the Bible, not for the first time, she saw things she had never been able to see before. Colm claimed she was reading it for the first time with spiritual eyes. Whatever the phenomenon, it pleased her immensely.

She was getting heartily tired of the engine's mindless noise. "Anything I can send you from the big city?"

He shook his head. "You sure you want me to keep Peter's Bibles?"

"Absolutely. He can't read, apparently. And if he does regain enough mental capacity to read, we'll celebrate by getting him one of those big print editions. I'm glad his old Bibles are getting good use."

"So's yours; I saw the marker in it. That pleases me."

She smiled and felt her ears grow warm. What a childish thing! "Remember I posted some letters just before I left?"

He nodded.

148

"One was to my parents in San Francisco, telling them what little I know so far. They liked Peter so much—they're going to be heartbroken. And the other was to the Kerns. I asked them to box up the library—all of it—and send it to you."

His head snapped around to stare at her. "You need them. You have to read and grow, too."

"You know how I love books. I'll accumulate a new library in no time. It's amazing how fast books multiply. Like rabbits. And I'm just starting out with God—brand new. It'll take me a long time to grow into Peter's theology books, but you're ready for them now. Besides, also, I'll be in a city where books are easily available. You don't have much selection in Coober Pedy." She paused. "Although I did see a collection of William Henry Lawson's works, so they can't be too ignorant."

"Still—" He drove this motor car with the same easy grace he drove Jewel. His arms hung relaxed before him, draped like bunting between his shoulders and the wheel. "Make sure I have an address for you. When you want some particular book, I'll send it to you."

"All right." Polly yearned for the silence Jewel provided. She much preferred a soft clop-clop and gentle creaking to this incessant BLIGGA-BLIGGA-BLIGGA-BLIGGA.

"You know?" Colm shifted in his seat. "I see a lot of good coming out of these last six months."

She stared at him again. This was the first time she could ever remember that he had initiated a conversation, except with David. "Meeting each other, you mean? Our lives aren't turning out fairy-tale lovely, are they?"

"Fairy tales are for children, remember? And not the army."

Polly almost laughed. When Colm pronounced the words they came out "furry tiles." She just now realized how accustomed she was to his thick accent, and how she now translated his words into her kind of English more or less automatically. Five years in Australia she constantly said "Sorry?" to request a repeat, and he had attuned her ear to the speech in half a year. "When I think about it, I'm glad I met you. Meeting and losing you is still better than never having known you at all."

"Yuh, that. I agree. More important to me is that you know the Lord now. Far and away that's most important. And you're stronger now. Able to take over Peter and handle all the decisions for both of you. It's a big job. I don't think you could've done it six months ago."

"I never thought of that. You're right. But you! You lost your horse, sold your saddle, gave away your opal and worked half a year for virtually no pay. It hasn't been a very good time for you. Unprofitable, to say the least."

The corners of his mouth kinked up into the most curious smile. "Ah, Polly, I've profited more than you'll ever know. Meeting you, as you say. Growing in the Lord. I'd been shirking my responsibility, you see. Some people accept Christ and then stay with older Christians. They're discipled, is the word. But if other people don't disciple you, you still have the responsibility to grow on your own. I wasn't doing that until I was stuck in one spot with a whole theology library. Best thing could've happened to me. There're other things, too.

"When I first met you, I didn't know if I was coming in or going out. All crossed tracks, wandering, aimless. Drifting, just like David. God turned me around and set me in a straight line again. And He showed me how strong I can be when it's Him I'm serving."

"How strong you can be?"

"Resisting temptation. The temptation to sway you away from doing the right thing; talk you into shedding Peter and marrying me. Believe me, I considered it. But I know you're doing what God wants, and it took a strong, hard rein on my heart to accept it. Then there's the temptation of you. Yourself. You're a beautiful woman, inside and out. It wasn't just temptation to sin. It was temptation to lust; wanting you, thinking about you in the wrong way. Daydreaming. That was hardest of all. And I know I can't let my guard down. Look what happened to King David back in Second Samuel. He let his guard down and paid for it the rest of his life. With God's help I can—"

"But the temptation's leaving."

"The woman's leaving, not the memory of her."

They came bouncing out of a sandy wash and up over a little rise. There was the railroad in the distance ahead. A little clot of ramshackle buildings grew steadily larger as the motor car approached. Polly recognized an outhouse (which Colm would be quick to refer to as a dunny), a chicken coop, some sort of horse shed and a little square building. Off beyond the tracks a few humpies dotted the barren dirt.

They chugged into the vast and vacant railyard and Colm let the motor die. The sudden silence made Polly's ears ring a moment. He looked around. "Not quite the size of Melbourne yet."

"But growing." Polly pointed to a pile of lumber and the framing for a second dunny.

Colm set her bags beside the tracks. Polly wandered off to the little square shack that ought serve as both home and office for the stationmaster. A hasp and wooden peg held the door closed from the outside. Nobody home.

Colm scanned the beaten dirt all around. "The stationmaster's either Aborigine or half-caste. Looks like they all went off on walkabout." Casually he pulled the wooden peg and pushed the door open. "Oughta be a schedule around." He disappeared inside—disappeared literally into darkness, for the building had no windows.

Polly peered into the gloom and could see very little.

151

Colm came back outside and fastened the door behind him. "Train's by in less than two hours, assuming they're anywhere near on time."

"Mmm." She wandered off to the tracks and studied the curious curled clips holding the rails to the ties. They used plain old spikes back home in America. Home. This was home now. She tried not to think about that other home from the past and concentrate on this one. The flies were especially bad today. They distracted her as she constantly shooed them from around her face.

She tried not to think of the heavy problems awaiting her at the south end of this railroad line. She tried not to think about the rangy, capable man she was leaving behind. Once in awhile she would cast a furtive glance his way. He either stood about in his normal state of slack repose or fiddled with Louise's car. He checked the tires, peered under the bonnet wiggling wires, and filled the petrol tank from cans in the back.

She saw the train in the north eventually, only a few minutes later than schedule. It was simply a dark dot at the apex of the converging tracks.

Colm was leaning now against the shady wall of the station house. She walked over to him.

"I have no idea what my expenses will be in Melbourne, but I'm sure I won't need what's in the account now. Feel free to use it to develop your claim."

"I'll keep a close record. And if you do find yourself short, I'll wire you whatever you need."

She nodded and smiled. "I'm glad to hear you talk like that. You sound confident you'll do well."

"Hargreaves introduced me to a fellow who's been digging awhile. They were showing me what looks promising and what doesn't. That hole I'm chipping away at looks good. I found out I wasn't the only one wanted the hole, either. Some fellow named Leadbetter wanted to buy it but the gent didn't want to sell to him. Didn't like him personally. Sold to me instead. So if this Leadbetter liked the claim it's probably got a lot of promise. He apparently has a good eye for that sort of thing, according to the locals."

"I hope your luck is changing."

"Not luck. Providence."

"Providence." She could hear the train. "It takes two to start the car up easily. Shall I help?"

" 'Preciate it." He lurched erect and ambled over to the machine. Polly climbed into the seat as Colm inserted the crank up front.

The train was halfway here now, no longer just a dot. Colm took a minute to step out onto the tracks and wave his hat mightily back and forth. He returned to the car and gave the crank a twist as Polly manipulated the mysterious knobs on the dash. She had no idea what a throttle did or did not do. The car sighed, belched and snubbed their efforts. Another crank, more fiddling—trembling with exertion the motor stuttered and picked up its steady BLIGGA-BLIGGA-BLIGGA-BLIGGA.

The train was slowing. Would it have slowed here had Colm not flagged it? Who knows what trains do when the stationmasters go off on walkabout. What a strange and wonderful country.

The dusty steam engine pulled alongside the square hut and sighed weightily. There was only one passenger car and several boxy freight cars.

Polly stood before Colm and had to force herself to look at him. "This is the most difficult thing I will ever do in my life."

Colm laid a hand on each of her shoulders and squeezed. "I'm proud of you. God bless you. I know He will." The luminous gray eyes were clouding up. "G'bye." He wheeled abruptly and climbed into the motor car. Louise's motor car.

They watched each other a final long moment as Polly paused beside the train.

A conductor of some sort picked up her bags. "Anyone else, marm?"

"Not that we've seen." She allowed him to give her

153

a hand up the steps. She found a seat facing backward at the windows on Colm's side. She wiped the glass hoping to see out better, but all the dust was outside. Through the fuzzy tan haze she watched Colm turn the wheel. Louise's car swung out in a wide circle as her own rail car jerked and began to move. There went the motor car off along the track toward Coober Pedy. And here went the rail car south toward Adelaide and Melbourne.

Her life was draining, emptied like a bucket with a hole. She felt so weary and despondent she was past weeping. She forced herself to smile at the older couple across from her. They smiled and nodded in return. The lady wore the usual black dress and floppy hat, and the gentleman was well turned out. They appeared prosperous.

"Are you going to Adelaide, Miss?" the lady asked politely.

"Melbourne, eventually."

"Oh, I hope you're not in a grand rush to get there. We hear Murray Bridge is out and just now being repaired."

"No, I'm in no rush," Polly murmured. "The man I'm meeting doesn't know I'm coming."

He doesn't even know.

She sent her mind on to other things. "That's a lovely piece you're wearing, madame, that sapphire. Is it local?"

"Oh, yes. The stone is from Queensland, up behind Brisbane, and my husband here fashioned the setting. He's a jeweler."

"Really." Polly looked at him a moment and liked his jolly blue eyes. "A gentleman came to my husband's farm last fall quite ill. In payment for our hospitality, he insisted we take *this*." She dug her opal out of her handbag and extended it. "Can you recommend a setting for it?"

The gentleman took her opal—the opal—and twisted it this way and that, admiring the fire. "Gorgeous," he

154

purred. "Perfect." He handed it back to her and whipped a card from his pocket. "As my wife mentioned, the bridge is out. Passengers are waiting in Adelaide until they can go on, as will you. Come to my shop at this address. I'd like to show you some possibilities."

"Thank you." She dropped the gem back into her handbag. "Thank you—" she glanced at his card— "Mr. Chambers."

They fell into conversation then, talking long hours and saying little of import. She learned all about the general business climate and about the gem business in particular; she would have to write some of these points to Colm. She heard about the grandchildren and the fine weather this time of year in Adelaide.

Polly did not intend to tell them about herself, but by the time darkness fell and weary travelers one by one dozed off, scrunched in their seats, she had dumped her whole sorry tale upon these two strangers. Somehow she felt better for the telling of it, but Mrs. Chambers had been reduced to tears, even though Polly said nothing about Colm—her love that would never be. The husband recommended moving from Melbourne to Adelaide and spent half an hour extolling the superior virtues of quiet, elegant gentle Adelaide over bustling, frantic Melbourne.

Polly spent nearly ten days in Adelaide as it turned out. The railroad had quite a back-up of passengers and freight, and because freight brings the higher revenue, freight was the first to fill the trains when service was at last restored. Polly didn't mind. Mr. Chambers was right about this town. Perhaps Peter would do better here, in a peaceful little cottage on one of these back streets. Polly left Adelaide reluctantly.

With her came her opal in a lovely new setting. Mr. Chambers had charged not much more than the cost of materials. He said the gold in the mounting had come from Kalgoorlie. Nothing less than native gold would do for this lovely stone, he said. He also provided a fine gold chain, from which he twice took links until the stone hung in the perfect spot below the hollow of her throat. It was custom work in every way.

She regretted leaving the Chambers, not because of the jeweler's professional service but because they were so warm and friendly. Polly needed warmth and friendship. On the long train ride down to Melbourne she reflected how many people in this sprawling land displayed that same warmth. Australia was booming, as banker Hollis had said. But the lovely land was not in the least losing its old, homey, cheerful friendliness.

The train pulled into Rockbank station in an afternoon and, huffing and puffing, reached Melbourne by evening. Electric lights had replaced gaslights through nearly all the city. The city glittered like the sky in her father's telescope, yet all these stars gleamed close enough to touch. She thought briefly of all the changes she had experienced in her lifetime—aeroplanes, electricity made common, motor cars. And her parents had seen far greater changes.

The aged rail car slowed, lurched, rocked, jerked, halted. Along with dozens of others, she stood and stretched and walked the narrow passageway to the doors. She stepped from stuffy warmth to cool evening breeze. Melbourne.

I'm here, Peter. At last I'm here.
Goodbye, Colm.

CHAPTER 15

MELBOURNE, THE BRAIN AND heart of Australia, big, bustling, booming, would be the nation's capital for only a few more years. Even now, builders were raising a brand-new capital city at Canberra between Melbourne and Sydney. But this city would not be the least bit destitute when her government offices left. So many commercial and financial interests called Melbourne home that she would hardly feel the excision.

All this was very nice for prosperous Melbourne, but it left Polly in a fine muddle. Polly had been born and raised in a city—San Francisco—but this beehive left her confused and lost. The morning sun cowered behind block upon block of towering buildings, some of them six or seven stories tall. They frowned at her, alient giants. Polly learned from her hotel clerk that the army hospital was only eleven blocks away.

But she would not walk there today. She would go tomorrow. In her good black dress she walked down the street until she found the sign she wanted. For the first time since coming to Australia, Polly entered a hair-styling salon.

"Yes?" An extremely crisp and stylish lady smiled at her from behind the counter.

"Tomorrow I shall rejoin my husband after a long absence. We'll be leaving the farm to take up life in town and I want to exchange this dowdy farm look for a more urbane appearance."

"I see! I'm so happy for you and your husband." The woman came sweeping around the counter. Her eyes shone with the eagerness of a sculptor given a new lump of clay. "Rest assured you'll be stunning. And may I compliment your lovely dress. This way."

Polly let herself be ushered through a curtain into the mysterious inner sanctum where dreams are polished and, in theory at least, dog biscuits are transformed into cookies.

Three hours later she paid her bill and stepped out into the streets of Melbourne a brand-new woman. Curious, this: she seemed to stand taller. She certainly felt taller, and sophisticated, too. Suddenly Melbourne did not seem nearly so intimidating.

She patted the back of her head. Her hands trembled, confused because the thick bun was gone. And oh, how she loved these loose, saucy little curls.

She ate lunch in a restaurant with real glamour, not the phony, pretentious airs of Armand's.

She spent an hour choosing just the right little hat to go with the dress. She purchased gloves to hide her work-worn hands. She spent another half hour picking out the right shoes—city shoes, with hard steep heels. She might have bought a new purse as well, but she could find none roomy enough to carry all the things she would bring to the hospital tomorrow.

Finally she bought a bag of popcorn with which to bribe the pigeons and one white cockatoo in the park near the hotel. She realized with a smirk that her concern was not for the birds; like a schoolgirl, she was placing herself on display before the world.

The hospital. Tomorrow. So Peter recognized no one. Therefore, it would not matter whether Polly looked

158

like the bride of old or whether the world saw a modern woman who would wear well this smart black dress.

She could not sleep that night. All her doubts and worries came sneaking in through the darkness to destroy her rest. She felt an overwhelming sense of loss. She felt too weak, too feeble to handle the enormous task ahead. So many years of emptiness faced her.

And yet, she didn't really know that. Perhaps Peter might emerge from his dark cloud. Or he might—

Tomorrow.

Tomorrow took weeks to arrive. Finally the sun slipped a shaft through her hotel window as honeyeaters clambered all over the tree outside.

She dressed with care and paused a few moments to survey the urbane new Polly in the mirror. She felt new. Different. What a change a haircut can make!

And yet it was not the hairstyle working this change. Back in San Francisco she had suffered no lack of confidence. On the voyage to Australia, in her marriage to Peter, she had suffered no feelings of uncertainty. And then, the self-confidence had somehow trickled away during those years on the farm as she waited. Had the isolation sapped her? Had the stodgy old granny clothes somehow stolen her faith in herself? No matter. The old feeling was returning, the feeling that she could handle, somehow, whatever the world dished out. The feeling had begun quietly, almost unnoticed, several months ago. Now here it was even stronger than before. The doubts of the night before were gone.

And yet she had modernized her appearance only yesterday. It could not be the new woman in the mirror who wrought this change. Her appearance was not the cause of her new self-confidence, it was the effect. She was the old Polly reborn.

Reborn! Yes, and more than reborn, the Polly she was now was infinitely more than the old Polly. She was the new Polly plus God. He was part of her. He

159

strengthened her. He filled in what she lacked. Polly Chase now had far deeper resources than just Polly Chase. Together she and God could take on the world . . .

. . . and win!

She sat by the window a few minutes, watching the patterns of light and shadow in the tree. A nervous noisy miner joined the honeyeaters momentarily and left again. A little fairy wren came hopping across the tree in search of tiny somethings in the branch bark. His brilliant iridescent blue flashed in the light-shadow patterns like that opal.

That opal.

She brought the opal out of its little velvet case. Freed from darkness it caught the window light and flashed its fire. She placed it around her neck. She had taken a course in literary symbolism. What did blue mean? Purity. Truth. God.

What an interesting quirk of fate. Colm Stawell had borrowed Peter's library to disciple himself to Peter's God. Colm Stawell had given Polly Peter's God. Because of Colm, Peter's God was now Polly's after so many years when she had sat in darkness. In ignorance.

She spent the next quarter hour in prayer, at times with her eyes closed and at times watching the sunflecks dance through the tree branches outside her window. She was delighted and just a little amazed that she could now commune comfortably with a God she had not even dreamt of before. He was a Person. He was here now, and He loved her.

She left the room eventually, strengthened. Ready. This was the day. She would need all the strength God could give her today. She ate breakfast quickly and started out on the years-long walk to the veterans hospital.

She had to ask directions twice to get there.

Finally here was the place, a great, gray box of a building. She hesitated only a moment to study the flat bleak walls, the enormous, morose, forbidding doors.

Was the inside as heartless and dull as the outside? She took a deep breath and climbed the outside stair with feet getting heavier step on step.

Spacious and sterile, the lobby was unrelieved by either soft lines or smiling people. An older couple sat on a bench, waiting apparently, as empty of face as the lobby was empty of cheer.

Polly crossed to what must be the reception desk. She made a smile. "My name is Polly Chase. Mrs. Peter Chase." Let the letter do the introductions. She passed the army's wrinkled-ironed note across to the lady and waited patiently as it was read.

The woman would not meet Polly's eyes. "Just a moment, please." She disappeared into a back room. Polly waited. She of all people knew about waiting.

A woman in a white pinafore and a strange little cap came pushing through a double door beyond the desk. Her white dress stopped halfway down her shins. Polly reminded herself that this was modern, progressive Melbourne.

"Mrs. Chase? Margaret Blanchard, C-wing supervisor. Come this way, please." She held the swinging door open for Polly. As Polly passed, she purred, "My, that's a lovely dress, Mrs. Chase. Quite tasteful."

"Thank you." Polly gripped her handbag tighter.

Mrs. Blanchard guided her along sterile flat gray halls, past sterile, endless, identical dark brown doors. Peter was little more than a vegetable? No wonder! P. T. Barnum himself would soon have lost his sparkle in such a depressing place.

A glimmer of brightness flickered in Polly's hopes. She would get Peter out of this drab institution; surround him with color and good cheer; lavish affection and attention upon him. He would almost certainly never return to normalcy, but he should surely respond at least a little to the stimulation and lovingkindness. He got none here, it was plain to see.

They climbed a hollow staircase at the far end. At the top landing Polly could look into a gloomy common

161

sitting room of some sort. A dozen men, faces pallid and drawn, sat about staring at nothing. Their faces and the walls looked just alike. Polly shuddered.

Mrs. Blanchard stopped at a plain brown door. "Now I must warn you, Jenny—may I call you Jenny?—he's not going to—"

"Not Jenny. It's Polly."

Mrs. Blanchard closed her mouth and just stood there, trapped by her slip of the tongue.

"Why Jenny?" Polly demanded.

"Among his effects is an intimate letter he started to write, apparently, and never finished. It begins 'Dear Jenny.' I assumed it would be you." She bit her lip. "Oh, Mrs. Chase, I'm terribly sorry! I erred badly!"

Jenny? Jenny! Polly had remained true to him all these years. Even when Colm lay in his cold dark loft and Polly lay in her cold dank bed, she had kept her marriage pure in thought as well as in deed. Where would he have found a Jenny? Some lost love preceding Polly, his ruined mind having skipped the middle years? A woman newly met somewhere between Corley Bore and the Dardanelles? Polly put it aside. She would explore the question some other time, if at all.

"It's quite all right, Mrs. Blanchard. Please don't feel badly. You were saying?"

Nonplussed, the woman cleared her throat and started over. "He's not going to recognize you. You must be prepared for that. His left arm is missing from the elbow down. That will come as a shock at first, no matter how carefully you rehearse your mind to receive it. And he's almost certainly lost weight since you last saw him. So steel yourself. The first jolt is always the worst."

Her eyes closed, Polly nodded. She would depend on her Lord to supply whatever strength she lacked. This was Peter, to whom she had bound herself for better or for worse. She accepted it. "Shall we go in?"

Mrs. Blanchard pushed the door open and stepped inside, leading the way. Their shoes clucked, muted, on the dull wooden floor of this long and open ward. Narrow iron pipe-frame beds lined the wall on either side. Water and heating pipes, painted the same dead gray as the walls, stretched the length of the ceiling, hung suspended, occasionally turned aside at a sharp, military right angle. The windows were set too high for anyone to reach, but it didn't really matter; they were too dirty to see through.

Empty men either lay on their sides on the beds or sat in chairs round about. Only a few of them made any note as Polly passed.

Mrs. Blanchard stopped and addressed a patient in a wheeled wooden chair. "Peter? Your wife is here. Polly Chase is here to visit you. It's Polly." She pronounced the name with an exaggerated emphasis.

The man sat all gray and cloudy beside his bed, dressed in the same colorless shirt and trousers all the other patients wore here. His face said what all those other men's faces said: "Nobody home."

Polly stared at him. She gaped. As the seconds ticked by, she could not speak.

Mrs. Blanchard squeezed her shoulder. "It's all right, Mrs. Chase. You're doing fine. It's all right."

"No!" Polly stammered. "No! It's not all right at all." Her lips stumbled as Mrs. Blanchard murmured something comforting. Panic rising in her breast, Polly pushed that hand off her shoulder. "It's all wrong! This man is not my husband. This is *not* Peter Chase!"

CHAPTER 16

"IN HERE, PLEASE." Mrs. Blanchard pushed a door open and ushered Polly through. It was a small office all a-jumble with file cabinets and stack upon stack of papers. From the midst of the clutter a harried-looking little man rose up at his desk.

He stretched out to extend Polly his hand. "Ian Stockley, the assistant director, Mrs. Chase. Do be seated."

Polly gave his hand a polite squeeze and plopped into the chair in front of his desk. Her knees were rubbery again. "Mrs. Blanchard told you my discovery."

"She says you feel the man called Peter Chase in our records is not the Peter Chase you married. She says you seem adamant." Mr. Stockley leaned back in his chair. "I'd like to point out that the mind plays some devastating tricks when it has received a shock, and even under the best of circumstances, seeing a man in Chaplain Chase's condition is a shock. Here is the mere shell of the warm and lively person you once knew. Now I don't—"

Polly could see where he was headed. She dug into

her purse as she cut him off. "Mrs. Blanchard. You've been on C wing several years, I take it."

"I was there when he came in, yes."

"Then you've known him over a period of time." Polly handed her the photos from her bag. "Did he ever resemble, even remotely, the man in these pictures?"

Mrs. Blanchard leafed from photo to photo—the wedding picture, the snapshot of them together at Wilson Promontory with the granite lighthouse in the background, the formal portrait they had made in Adelaide for Polly's friends back in the States. She flicked them over to look at the dates inked on the backs. She handed them to Mr. Stockley. "He's not the same man these pictures show."

A young girl knocked and entered timidly. Polly would have liked her short auburn hair more if it didn't remind her so much of Louise. She gave Mr. Stockley a bulky brown envelope. "Chaplain Chase's effects, sir."

He mumbled a thank you and dumped the envelope out on his desk.

Polly pulled out Peter's one letter written from Egypt and passed it across the desk. "Here's a sample of his writing. Does it match the unfinished letter Mrs. Blanchard mentioned?"

Mr. Stockton laid the two bits of paper side by side and pored over them. Mrs. Blanchard stood at his elbow craning her neck. "Oh my," she muttered. "Oh, my."

Mr. Stockley scratched his head and peered out over his glasses. "Knowing how the system operates, I would glibly say that a mix-up like this is impossible. And yet, your letter and photos prove otherwise."

Polly's firm resolve was dissolving. She tensed her arms and clasped her hands together. "I brought them along hoping to jog his memory. I hoped—" She stopped, lest she melt into tears. "Now I don't know what to do."

"Nor do I." Mr. Stockley whispered it again to himself. "Nor do I." He looked up at Mrs. Blanchard for help. She stepped back and crossed her arms, just as perplexed.

Polly could not depend on these two to solve her problem. They possessed a certain proprietary interest in the whole affair, but Peter Chase was not their kin. This was Polly's problem and she must take first responsibility for solving it. She hopped to her feet impulsively and paced to the far end of the room. She felt too numb sitting still. She was stopped short by piles of papers stacked on the floor.

She wished she could think more clearly. "When Peter arrived here—that is, the man with Peter's identification—I would assume others arrived with him. He wasn't alone?"

Mrs. Blanchard nodded. "Most probably he was part of a group. They almost always arrived by the boat load, as it were."

"Mr. Stockley, you feel the system would not permit the mix-up. If that's so, the mix-up occurred at the other end of the line, in Egypt or Europe or the Dardanelles, and probably on purpose."

"You're suggesting two parties, one of them Peter Chase, switched identities deliberately? I can think of no reason anyone would do that."

"Mr. Stockley, is there any way to tell who in this hospital might have been with Peter—I mean, that man—on the boat home, or in hospitals overseas?"

"Not without sorting through the files one by one to look at arrival dates."

Polly looked around in consternation at these acres of papers, at the general state of the filing system itself. "Would all the people in that man's group be in the same wing?"

"No." Mrs. Blanchard shook her head emphatically. "They were assigned whatever beds happened to be available at the time, hospital-wide. Some special cases, of course, such as those bound for the psychiatric ward, were limited, but that wouldn't be his case, I don't think."

"And he doesn't talk at all."

"Not a word."

Polly sorted through her thoughts out loud. "If that man is not Peter Chase, then someone else is. He's either dead, or here, or somewhere else. If he's dead or somewhere else, I suppose he's beyond finding. But if he's here—if he came home with this man—I mean, after all, the army thinks he's alive."

"The army also thinks this man is he." Mr. Stockley stood up. "If he's in this hospital, you're the one to identify him. The problem is exacerbated, of course, by the fact that so many of our patients have either died or been released. It's been a long time. Mrs. Blanchard, can your duties spare you?"

"My duties can wait. I'll go with her."

Mr. Stockley stood up. "If that man is not your Peter Chase, despite the serial number and the fact that his full name is identical with our records, then he is someone else. And we must find out who he is. Tour the wards. Look at men. If Peter Chase is here, find him."

"Thank you, Mr. Stockley." Polly gathered up her photos and letter and jammed them back into her bag as she followed Mrs. Blanchard out the door.

And the nightmare began.

They started systematically at the bottom of A wing, walking from ward to ward, from room to room. She looked at every haunted face. She asked every person capable of responding, "Did you know a Chaplain Peter Chase in the Mediterranean theatre?" Polly found herself incredibly depressed in minutes. How could Mrs. Blanchard work here for years?

Polly treated the pragmatic nurse to lunch and tea and off they went again. B wing; nothing. C wing; just that empty man with Peter's name. The horrid dream intensified as they walked the length of the psychiatric ward. So many wasted lives! Polly forced her mind to think of Colm, all healthy and strong and warm and alive—the antithesis of these wasted soldiers who had given more than their all for freedom.

"Let me see your face, please. Did you ever know a Chaplain Peter Chase in the Mediterranean theatre?"

Let me look at your hollow eyes and see Peter somehow.

They finished the interminable walk at 4:15 P.M.

Polly followed Mrs. Blanchard listlessly back to Mr. Stockley's office. Her voice as flat and gray as this whole oppressive building, Polly reported that the real Peter Chase did not live here. He was beyond finding.

She thanked both for their help, though she could not remember what she said even as she was saying it. Peter was not here. Her situation was neither better nor worse than it had been during her five years of waiting. No, that was not true. Her situation was infinitely worse.

As soon as the army ironed out their mistake, her paychecks would end. That desolated man in C wing, stripped of even this borrowed identity, would become a complete nonentity and Peter would be re-consigned to limbo. In America, one had to wait seven years before declaring a missing person dead. Was it seven in Australia, too? Seven years!

She walked out across the cavernous lobby. Those two older people were gone. Three young women had taken their places and borrowed their vacant stares.

"Mrs. Chase!" The clerk with short curly hair called from Mr. Stockley's doorway. "Please come."

Polly frowned. She had looked at every man there; she had asked every man. She returned as rapidly as her tired legs and aching feet permitted.

A tall heavy-set nursing sister was pushing a young man in a wheelchair through Mr. Stockley's office door. Vaguely, Polly remembered the man as from A wing— or was it B wing? That particular boy, if she recalled correctly, had at least a spark of light in his eyes when she talked to him. And he had professed no knowledge of a Chaplain Chase.

She followed the wheelchair into the office. The door clicked behind her.

The nurse, a take-charge sort of older woman, wiggled a finger toward Polly. "Here she is. Now tell her exactly what you told me."

"Polly Chase, right? Polly?" The young man raised a permanently crippled right arm to shake hands. Bent claw-shape and atrophied, the hand trembled. Polly noticed he had no legs.

Quickly she deliberately adjusted her attitude to the circumstance. She must be strong. She smiled, grasped the deformed hand firmly and shook. "Yes, it's Polly. How did you know?"

"Peter talked about you."

Her strength drained instantly. Peter. She glanced around rapidly, but Mr. Stockley beat her to it; he whipped his own chair out from behind his desk and pushed it under her. She flopped into it, then mustered the starch to perch closer to its edge. "You *did* know Peter! What is your name?"

"MacDonald. Bryan MacDonald. Your husband was a chaplain." He looked at her face briefly and studied the floor.

"Go on." The nursing sister poked him.

"The offensive at Gallipoli, early on. We were in the middle of it. One of our lads was wounded and Peter crawled out of the bunker under fire; tried to help the lad back to safety. The Turks got him—Peter, I mean—half blew his head off. And when all's said, the lad he tried to save died anyway.

"It was a black day, marm. It looked every minute like the Turks was gonna push us right into the sea. But worse was the fear we might be captured. Y'see, we heard a lot of stories about what the Turks did to captives. Atrocities, y'know?"

"I understand most of the stories were untrue. Just war rhetoric."

"Aye, but we didn't know that then, y'see. I had this buddy named Harry. Harry something. Wentz? Yair,

Wentz. My mind is a little slippery in spots since the war. Anyway, Harry was bitter scared of the Turks. Here we were in this trench, hiding behind sandbags, with a dead chaplain and a pile of dead buddies and all them Turks." Bryan's lower lip trembled. He paused, then continued.

"Harry remembered as how the Turks were terrible religious. Weren't Christian, of course, but religious in their own way. He opined maybe the Turks would go easier with a religious man—a man who wasn't directly carrying a rifle or fighting. Sounded logical at the time."

"He changed identities with Peter," Polly whispered. "Harry died that day and Peter lived on."

"That day, aye. But that night we got shelled. The Turks, they really like fireworks—all those lights exploding. A shell left Harry pretty much as you see him now. That's him in C wing. Harry."

"Why didn't you set the record straight? You knew the truth."

"Aye, but I was the only one who knew; oh, others woulda known before long, but I was the only one with Harry when he emptied pockets and all. I was gonna tell, but then I thought: Hey, Bryan, you know both these gents. Harry's got no next of kin, no responsibilities to no one. But Peter there, he has this bride back in New South Wales or wherever. Ah, marm, you shoulda heard him talk about you! The man was sunk in love deeper than an outback bore. You were already getting his paycheck; I knew about that arrangement. If he was known to be dead, the checks would stop. So I let it slide as it was. Harry being still alive, you'd still get your money and when Harry came home, you'd set the matter straight. And if Harry died, you got a few months' more checks, right? And nothing lost. No hurry telling the army about the switch. But then we were on the offensive again, and then we were pulling out, and I 'most forgot about it. So many ugly memories. It was just one more from the trenches, y'know?"

"Why didn't you tell me this when I talked to you earlier today?"

"I was afraid what they might do to me for keeping quiet so long. Then I figured, here sits old Bryan. What can they do to me that ain't done already? Right? So I told Sister Iron-stockings here and she brought me to Mr. Stockley."

Polly tried to speak and could not. She sat back in her chair and clamped her hands over her mouth trying to keep her sorrow at bay. It didn't work. Her eyes filled up and ran over. She could do nothing but let it come and hope it would not deteriorate into wild, uncontrollable sobbing.

Mr. Stockley sighed. "Thank you, MacDonald. So either the army or the postal service messed this one up. You failed to get word, Mrs. Chase, and I'm terribly sorry."

Polly stiffened her back and dragged her pieces back together. "The problem is partly mine. I should have inquired much sooner. I didn't know it could be done until a friend showed me how to go about it."

"MacDonald, you say he tried to rescue a fallen comrade. Would you say he acted heroically?"

"Too right, sir! Entitled to any kind of medal you wish to give him. Crawled out and never hesitated. Almost made it, too."

Mr. Stockley handed Polly his handkerchief, a thoughtful gesture for hers was soaked. "Mrs. Chase, will you return next Monday, please? I want to set some wheels in motion here; see what we can do about this."

"Certainly." Polly stood up. She stooped down again to eye-level with Bryan MacDonald. She squeezed his hand warmly. "Thank you for speaking out. I'm greatly indebted."

"Nae, marm, shoulda said something long ago. Never knew you hadn't heard, and Harry's in that other wing; never saw him. My sympathies. He was a sterling jack, your husband."

"Thank you." She stood up again and took her leave of the staff. She turned and walked out the varnished door, through the echoing lobby, out the pompous, whispering front doors and into late afternoon sun. She felt numb all over, as a foot feels when you've been sitting on it too long and it goes to sleep.

She walked aimlessly, mindlessly. She arrived eventually at a modest stone bridge. Under it coursed the Yarra, all beset by rock walls on both sides. She remembered the Yarra outside of town. The train taking her and Peter to their honeymoon down by Wilson Prom had traveled alongside the Yarra for a while. Outside town it flowed wild and free, uncorseted by these constricting walls. Was this pinched and domesticated stream the same lovely river that so lavishly spread itself out under the gum trees, and lingered in quiet, reflective little pools here and there along its way?

She turned aside and began following the riverwalls upstream. The waters were not just trammeled here, they were much dirtier than was the river outside of town.

Five years she had waited, doing little more than sitting and reading her books and magazines and tying lace. If Colm had not entered her life she would still be sitting there waiting, no doubt. And Harry would be sitting, also.

She passed a pretty little green park along the river shore and continued northeast. The sun was waning now, stuffing itself down behind those scowling city buildings. She left the river briefly to skirt some warehouses and rejoined it a block later. Colm. She thought of him sitting in the evening with his Bible in his lap. Then he would stand and fill the room with his stretching.

Already she had spent too much time in the south here. And there was much more left to do: straighten out the details of Peter's death, unsnarl all the legal tangles that accompany a matter like this. Was Colm married already to Louise? He really didn't seem to mind her moodiness; he seemed almost too ready to forgive her insane tantrums. He liked her much more than he would admit to Polly, obviously. And he clearly admired strong women; he had worked deliberately to make Polly stronger.

How long had she feared the possibility of widowhood? How many thousands of times had she pushed it to the back of her mind, had forcibly removed it from the list of possibilities? Now that it was a reality—*the* reality—she could not decide exactly how to deal with it. The very word *widow* seemed a term that could only apply to other women. Older women than she.

Widowhood. Such a hollow and despairing word. Hollow and despairing? What did Polly have in common with "hollow and despairing?" All those broken men she looked at today—now that was hollow and despairing. They had no hopes, no loved ones, no expectations. Most of them had no clear mind and almost none a whole body. Polly's situation was neither hollow nor despairing. She was still young; she had her good health. And at last she knew her exact situation—

widow—

and she could now get on with her life. She could step out with vigor and seize life now, after all the waiting.

Mr. Kern's leasehold included an option-to-buy clause. Polly could let him exercise that option. After death duties, she would still have enough money to establish herself in some town and live comfortably, at least for a while. She was young yet, though no spring chicken (make that "spring chook"). She would stay on here in Australia, for she liked the country and its far-ness.

The light was nearly gone now. She heard a train off to the left somewhere, so she turned north to a railway and followed it to Eltham Station. She would take the rail line back downtown to her hotel.

She had just missed a train and the next was not due for an hour and ten minutes, so she sat down on a slatted bench to wait. She was good at waiting, very good. The stationmaster turned on the electric lights above the platform. Amazing thing, electricity. Polly never did quite get the idea of how it worked; it constantly awed her.

Her jaw muscles tightened. Her eyes grew hot. Quietly, in the gathering darkness, Polly Chase began to weep. For that hour and ten minutes her grief poured out as wild and free as the upper Yarra, uncontained. On that railway station bench, she fell in love with Peter all over again, and grieved for him as though he were only a few days gone from her.

Peter.

Dear lost Peter, heroic to the end.

Peter.

CHAPTER 17

THE TRAIN CAR RATTLED. Its wheels argued with the tracks and clucked their tongues. The wind rushed whooshing past the open window. When you thought about it this train car was absolutely noisy, especially when compared with the silence of the flat open desert through which they were traveling. Polly leaned back in the leather seat. Her dress was sticking all wet wherever she touched. December was not quite mid-summer, technically speaking, but this far north "not quite" meant nothing. Heat was heat.

A fly buzzed in languid circles near the ceiling. Here they were, whipping along northward at perhaps twenty-five or even thirty miles an hour; yet the fly hung nearly motionless. Surely some law of physics covered the situation, but it was lost to Polly. Her father would know. She might try to remember to ask, next letter.

She wouldn't be writing again for a while, though. She had already asked him to send Colm some general astronomy books. She had explained to her parents all about poor Peter. She had sent them Peter's posthumous award for valor, for Peter's own parents were dead and hers regarded him as another son. She had not mentioned in the letter how she felt about Colm.

She had written to Colm, too, telling him about Peter. Then she had torn that letter up without mailing it. The letter she actually did mail said simply that she was returning alone to Coober Pedy and looked forward to seeing him there. She had wished him God's blessing on his digging and on his study. The second was by far the better letter. If he were still unattached, she would tell him all about Peter. If he were married now, or committed to another, she would say Peter was still in the veterans hospital. Then they would part forever, and Colm none the wiser that the derelict young man in C ward was a bogus Peter.

Far out on the desert to the west, three or four humpies broke the level line. Where was David? Polly more than half suspected he was by now in Coober Pedy, if not with Maggie somewhere along the Larrapinta. The Larrapinta was a long, long river; how would he ever find Maggie, anyway? Polly had heard stories about mulga wire, the mental telepathy with which some Aborigines communicated across distances of many miles. Her father refused to believe in it. Polly was not so certain, having now met an Aborigine or two. She might ask Colm about it. He would know if mulga wire really worked, and if it were a common gift of Aborigines or whether only a privileged few practiced it.

A smooth and dapper sort of fellow appeared by her shoulder. "May I sit there?" He nodded toward the seat facing hers.

"Certainly." She smiled politely and returned to her study of that straight line marking the horizon.

He pulled a folded newspaper out from under his arm as he sat. "I was at the back of the car sandwiched between two chronic cigar smokers. Don't like cigar smoke all that much."

"Me either."

"Going to Alice?"

"Coober Pedy."

"Where? Oh. Opal camp. Business?"

"Business and pleasure. Tend to business with the dry goods merchants and visit a friend. You're going to Alice?"

"Alice, opal camp sooner or later—several places. My employer stores up things for me to do, to make the trip pay for itself."

"And your employer is . . . ?"

"Wire service." He grinned and lost five years off his appearance. "I like to think of myself as a reporter, but I do mostly mop-up. You know, follow up on stories after the excitement is past. Like the excitement in the opal camp. I'll miss that, but I'll hit town there in a few days to make sure there are no loose ends worthy of one more story."

"Excitement? In Coober Pedy?" Polly found herself snickering. She could not imagine anything more exciting than the tin sheeting blowing off someone's shed in a storm.

"The murder trial. Hanging's tomorrow morning. Some gent killed his lover over money."

Polly wagged her head. "Isn't it terrible what greed does to a person?"

"Too right! And the pity of it was he needn't have done it. A few days after the deed, he struck quite a find of opals in his dig. Could've been wealthy without doing the old bat in. If he'd only waited a few weeks."

"Bad timing."

"Isn't it, though?"

Polly smiled inside. Poor Colm, too, had suffered bad timing, and through no fault of his own.

The young man snapped his paper open and studied empty space a few moments. "They say that the lower classes suffer not so much from underprivilege as lack of judgment. Not everyone says that, of course, but it's a theory that's been bandied about. This fellow claims innocence, yet there's all the evidence. So many things he could have done—" The fellow lowered his paper a little. "I'm speaking indelicately, but there's so much he could have done more covertly, tactfully, if you will, to cover his tracks. Fighting with the woman in public, things like that; not conducive to a quiet little murder. But then, you see, the fellow was a drifter. Sundowner. No-hoper. Had he been a man of means—" The paper came up again.

". . . he would have been much more discreet." Polly finished the thought. "Perhaps even wise enough to wait until his opal strike."

"Exactly. Bad judgment, beginning to end. Do you read mystery novels?"

"No. I tried a few and didn't like them all that well." Polly thought about the words this young man had just used. Drifter. Sundowner. She had applied them to Colm at one time. And yet he was none of that. How does one tell a genuine no-hoper from a fellow simply down on his luck (or down on his providence, in Colm's case)?

Tosh! There's no such thing as "down on your providence." God's providence is always perfect. Polly did not the least understand why He did certain things as He did, but she entertained every confidence that He did them for a good reason. The sticky little verse in Romans was true, after all, even if she could not always say why or how.

"Sorry," the young man said. "Got off on the case and lapsed my manners. My name is Edgar Seavers, how do you do?"

"Polly Chase. Pleased to meet you." She watched the spinifex speed by outside and remembered wading through it in search of Maggie, oh so long ago.

The newspaper was crackling, wilting slowly in Mr. Seavers's hands. Rather it was the hands themselves wilting. The newspaper crumpled into a forgotten wad in his lap and he was staring at her intently, fascinated. Polly noted his eyes matched his hair color, a rich chocolate brown. The eyes had grown to twice their normal size.

"Mr. Seavers. Might you look off somewhere else, please?"

"And an American accent, too! Madam, can you prove you're Polly Chase?"

"Of course I can. What—?"

"And your husband's name?"

"Peter."

"And you must tell me, Mrs. Chase, whom you are visiting in the opal camp. Please?" There was an urgency to his voice, a tinge of fear.

The fear infected Polly, it was so strong. She felt a lightning-sharp tickle of excitement. "Colm Stawell. Spelled S-T-A-W-E-L-L, though you wouldn't know it to hear him pronounce it. Why are you staring?"

"They never found the body," he purred. He exploded. "Of course they never found the body! What a break! What an unimaginable find! Why, you could launch my whole career; I can make a name for myself as a journalist just with this one—" He leaped to his feet. "Conductor!"

The black-suited gentleman came trotting down the aisle. "What's wrong?"

"Where's the closest, quickest stop to the opal fields?"

The conductor studied Mr. Seavers as if the young man had spiders in his hair. "Manguri's closest, but there's hardly anyone there. Once you leave the train, you're stranded. Anna Creek is a hundred miles, but there's usually a lorry or two about, horses, a camel train."

"Telegraph?"

"Supposed to be."

"Thank you, sir!" The young man flopped back into his seat.

The conductor wandered back up the aisle, muttering about people who drink too much on railroad trains.

"Enough of these theatrics, Mr. Seavers! Begin at the beginning."

He rubbed his face in his hands. "I still can't believe

179

this. A man and woman, apparently not married to each other, arrived at the opal fields. According to witnesses their horse and wagon was the woman's, as was all the money. She established a hefty bank account in her own name and rented a postal box; obviously intending to stay awhile.

"Witnesses testified that on at least one occasion this woman and he were yelling and throwing things in his hotel room. A regular knock-down blue going. Soon thereafter, the woman appears at the bank all puffy-eyed and distressed—under coercion, you see. She had the bank add the man's name to the account, so that he could draw on it at will. And he did, too, quite heavily. A week later a parcel comes for him, but the things in it have her name in them."

"Books and things. Mr. Kern was prompt."

"That's right! The return address was August Kern." The boy grinned broadly. "Mrs. Chase, you are the only person who could have known that. It was in our reporters' notebooks but never in the papers." He rubbed his hands gleefully.

"Go on!"

"He drives out of town with her in a borrowed motor car, and returns without her. From then on he's using her horse and wagon. When she doesn't show up, authorities get naturally suspicious and arrest him."

"But there isn't enough real evidence to—No body—"

"Right! But the authorities weren't too worried about the lack of a corpse. Some of those mines are ten stories deep. He could have dropped a body down any of a hundred shafts and it would probably never be found. Or bury it anywhere along the track to the railroad. It was the witnesses that clinched the case."

"Witnesses! To what?"

"Well, there's the girl who owns the motor car. She swore he got real ugly with her and she loaned it out of fear. And that she'd heard him threaten to kill the woman more than once. Apparently she traveled part-way in their party or something."

"Witnesses. You said witnesses. Who else?"

"Just a moment." Mr. Seavers dug into his coat pocket and whipped out a small notebook. He leafed from page to page. "Here it is. A Myron Leadbetter. The other witness's name was—"

"Louise Flett. Go on."

"Yes." He looked at her a moment. "Mr. Leadbetter testified that the fellow roughed her up several times, out by the ridges. Where 'by the ridges' is I don't know as yet. On one occasion, apparently, the argument was over money. The defendant felt the woman was being too niggardly in her dole."

"Why, such a thing never happened. And what was the defendant's testimony?" The enormity of all this was crushing Polly's insides and clouding her mind. She could not think.

"Oh, claimed he didn't do it, of course. Claimed he put her on the train to Melbourne, was all. Then the prosecution countered that if she intended to go to Melbourne, she wouldn't have opened a postal box or bank account. And no one could come up with any witnesses at the rail stop."

"They were off on walkabout. When was the trial?"

"Last week. Didn't last long."

"And you said the hanging is in the morning? You mean *that* hanging?"

"Dawn. I'm not sure we can get there by then. But we'll wire ahead and have them stay the execution; tell them the body's alive and well and on the way."

"Why didn't they check with anyone in Melbourne? Colm knew I'd be at the veterans hospital."

The young man sat back and studied her a moment. She might have trouble thinking, but he was obviously galloping along in top form upstairs. "I smell a fast shuffle, as you say in the States. It doesn't look that anyone took a lot of trouble on Stawell's behalf. Does he have enemies?"

181

"Colm? Hardly. He's a fine Christian man who treats everyone fairly."

Mr. Seavers laughed. "Everyone, indeed." He flipped through a couple other pages in his notebook. "The prosecution established Stawell's reputation as a low-class in part by showing the fellow had an unhealthy association with blacks. That's what it says here. Have no notion what a healthy association with blacks might be."

"Local blacks? Or an Aborigine named David?"

"Nothing in my notes. But it was one of the points made against him."

"Enemies. I vaguely recall Colm mentioning—and I think now the name he mentioned was Leadbetter, or close to it—that he bought his claim from a fellow who had been offered a sum by a Leadbetter and refused. The owner—the prior owner, that is—didn't like Leadbetter and wouldn't sell to him, so he sold to Colm instead."

The young man's eyes brightened. The smile on his face told Polly that she might not like mystery novels, but this fellow certainly did. "The question becomes, Mrs. Chase; To whom does the claim revert after this Stawell is swinging so wild and free? After the hemp, who mines his opals?"

Polly's hands were shaking. It was good she was sitting; her knees were melting into pools of uselessness again. It was not just Colm's lethal predicament. It was not just the horrid injustice of all this, and the wholesale greed surfacing. Louise was in it. Louise didn't care all that much about owning an opal mine. She wanted the miner.

That poor puppy flashed through Polly's memory. Destroying a puppy to keep it from falling into black hands was one thing, but lying in a court of law was quite another. Or was it?

If Louise would go to those lengths to ruin Colm, that must mean he had refused her! Louise was spoiling Colm for anyone else because she could not have him, and if she couldn't have him, no one else would, either. She had said so! Colm had rebuffed her, apparently permanently and without hope he would change his mind. The thought thrilled and strengthened Polly.

"This is so fast. I've been gone from there less than eight weeks. Why such a hurry?"

"If it is a claim grabbing, they want it over with before you show up, perhaps. Besides," the young man flipped his notebook shut, "you know how it is with the law. If you have a lot of money they dawdle about forever. If you're lower class—and they took great pains to paint this Stawell as a loser—they don't waste the time on you."

The fellow pondered the scenery a moment. "Know where we are?"

"About. We'll de-train at Anna Creek, get a telegram through and then follow it. We'll make it." She locked his eyes with her own.

"We'll make it." He said it firmly, without reservation. He fumbled for a pencil and snapped the notebook open again. "Now tell me what you know about this Leadbetter fellow and the Flett girl. Stawell, too. All of them."

"Yes. Just wait until I tell you about Louise Flett."

Oh, Colm! We're coming! I don't know how we'll manage it, but God is with us. We'll get there on time!

I'm coming, Colm!

CHAPTER 18

OBVIOUSLY THE CONDUCTOR INTENDED to wait until the train stopped before opening the door. Polly was not about to lounge around that long. She pushed past him as Edgar yanked the door wide. They were halfway across the beaten yard before the car's brakes quit squealing steel on steel.

She slammed into the little square office, breathless from the sudden exertion. "I must send a telegram immediately to Coober Pedy!"

"The opal fields? Now?"

"Surely there's a line open."

"Now and then. Not now. Down, somewhere along the track. Mail goes out Friday, though. That'll get there by Monday or Tuesday."

"This is a matter of life and death. I must get word there instantly!"

He gave her a no-use-reasoning-with-women scowl. "How fast can you run?"

Angry beyond words, she spun on her heel and very nearly ran over Edgar as she boiled out the door. Edgar Seavers loved to argue, but it did him no good. She could hear them in there. Frustrated, she stood in the late afternoon sun. What to do? What to do? *Lord, Colm is your servant and I can save him. Guide me! Show me!* She inhaled deeply. She was raging now and neither praying nor thinking rationally. She must think and pray both!

BLIGGA-BLIGGA-BLIGGA-BLIGGA came one of those trucks Colm fancied. The word "White" was scrolled catty-cornered up its radiator grill. It chugged over to a baggage car and coughed to a stop.

"That truck!" Polly cried. "Come on, Edgar!"

She ran the length of the yard and hailed the driver before he could climb down off his seat. "Wait!" She parked squarely in front of him as she dug into her handbag. "I want to hire your truck. How fast can you get to Coober Pedy?"

"The opal fields?"

She pulled out a twenty-pound note. "Edgar, how much do you have to wave before him? How many of these you earn depends upon how quickly you can get us there. It's an emergency—an extreme emergency— and we'll pay well."

"Well, ah, expenses you know: petrol, some oil for the crankcase; and tires ain't cheap."

"Expenses plus our fee, if you get us there on time."

The young man studied her note and the money in Edgar's hand behind her. He glanced at the parcels being unloaded beside the railcar and back at the bait. His face burst into a wide grin. "Hop in! Ye want it fast? Fast it is!" He chortled, "This is gunner be one fun ride, clear to the opal fields."

"Do you have enough fuel with you?"

"Aye, mum, but not enough to get back on. There's petrol there?"

"There is. Let's go." She clambered up into the seat beside him and Edgar squeezed in against her.

"Ye got baggage?"

"It can wait. Go!"

He looked at her a moment. "Ye know, mum, it really must be an emergency." He shoved the gear

185

stick here and there; the truck lurched into motion. Polly's head snapped back; she grabbed for anything to hold on to, but there was nothing.

Squeezed between Edgar and this bumpkin, she bounced pretty much vertically only. The rutted road stretched away before them, constricting down to that familiar little point on the horizon.

There was a wild exhilaration to this particular ride, much more than on that ride here with Colm. The thrill went beyond the bucketing and bouncing. It went beyond the solid thrum of the motor, or the speed. They were bound on an adventurous and critical mission, a race against time and greed and evil in the heart of a twisted auburn-haired girl.

The sun set almost directly ahead of them. The young man squinted, half blind. "My name's Herbert Towne. I own this truck, y'know. Bought it freehold after the war. Make a pretty good living hauling. Going outback here, if it breaks down I'm days reaching town, days getting it fixed; lose money if it's outta service too long. I'm taking a risk, y'know."

"And we surely appreciate it!"

She glanced up at Edgar. The urbane young reporter was having the time of his life, chasing after a marvelous story in such a grand vehicle.

Bang!

The truck lurched alarmingly sideways and bumped to a stop.

"Arrgh! Just when we was getting on so well!" Herbert and Edgar slid off the seat to study the front wheel, Herbert holding a light, a broom torch.

Polly looked but had no idea what she was looking at. "Will this take long?"

"Fifteen, twenty minutes."

"Can I help?"

"Fetch the other spanner in the toolbox there. Ed, you hold this."

It took Polly awhile to get the toolbox open; stronger fingers than hers had closed it. Here was the spanner in question, she supposed; a wrench elsewhere in the world.

Herbert and Edgar were grunting together, so Polly held the torch. The driver caught his finger in the jack and yelped, shaking his whole hand vigorously.

"Fetch the petrol tin, Ed. Might's well fill it up while we're stopped."

Polly's stomach gurgled. She was outrageously hungry, for she hadn't eaten for—she calculated mentally—twenty-nine hours. Still this was no time to think of creature comfort. She would eat at Coober Pedy, in Barney's. With Colm. She put her thoughts to words. "When we get there, I'll treat you to the dinner of your choice."

Herbert grinned. "And I'm just hungry enough I'll let ye do that, too." He tossed his jack in the back—and froze. He stared at Polly. "The hanging! That's the emergency; the only thing going on in the opal camp. You two wanna get there for the hanging! Well ye aren't gonna; not by me!"

"What are you talking about?" Edgar, sounding irritable, was already up in the seat.

"I'm not that firing ready to watch a man stretch; 'specially not *that* man. I read in the papers what he said. Said he forgave the people who were doing this to him. He *forgave* 'em! Men he called his enemies. That doesn't sound like some murderer, and I for one don't care to stand there and watch him die!" He wheeled and strolled off.

Polly ran after him. "He isn't a murderer!" She wrenched Herbert around to face her. "I'm the victim! I'm Polly Chase."

He stared at her. "American accent! Hooey, lady! Why didn't you say so to start with?!" He grabbed her arm and practically bore her through the air to the truck. With a massive shove he heaved her up onto the seat and scooted in beside her. The engine coughed and bellowed. "Electric starter!" He grinned. They were on their way.

The moon came up, and good thing; the feeble little lamps on this truck were not really bright enough to tell the driver anything about the road ahead. They saw kangaroos in the headlights twice and nearly struck one. Herbert talked for half an hour about how the kangas liked to hang around the roads, where run-off made the vegetation just a wee bit denser and greener. Polly saw no difference between the straggly roadside grasses and that farther off, but it didn't matter. She kept him talking to keep him alert.

Somewhere around midnight they passed an aboriginal campfire far off to the north. She wondered again where David might be.

Polly was able to tell Herbert and Edgar—especially young Edgar, for Colm's religious nature was already in his notebook—about Colm's spiritual walk. She explained at length the path taken, trusting Jesus Christ for eternal life, and thereafter pleasing God in thought and deed. She explained it as Colm had explained it to her more than once; service to God was not to bribe one's way into heaven; it was a gift in gratitude for heaven already won.

She found it easy talking about God now. So long she had shunned religion and now she found it bubbling out of her naturally. Peter would have been proud of her; Colm had already said he was.

At four in the morning they emptied the last petrol can into the tank. The countryside was becoming familiar now with its low flat ridges and endless expanse. The eastern sky turned murky gray and promised more light to come. Here was a small white cone, the sorry tombstone of a dead dream.

They were coming into the opal fields proper now. Myriad little cones stood out vividly in the dim predawn.

"Where will they be keeping him? Would you know?" Polly watched Harry Hacksaw's claim go by. They were nearly there now.

Edgar grunted as the truck bucked over a rut. "It's

getting close to first light. We'd better just look for the scaffold first and work backwards from there."

Polly snorted. "With so much of the town underground, the gibbet should be the tallest thing around." She frowned. "I smell something burning."

"Something hot. This crate'll hold together another couple miles. We'll make it." Herbert sounded grim.

"Cross your fingers," Edgar instructed.

"I'll pray instead, if you don't mind. It's certain to be more effective." Polly pointed wildly. "There! A little knot of people!"

"Aye, that's it." Herbert slammed both feet on the pedals as the motor sputtered and fluttered. Dirty smoke was creeping out from under the hood now. Herbert was nursing it along, coaxing, pleading; and the motor responded reluctantly. Finally, with a hiss and a snap, it died.

"Go! Run!" For lack of anything better to do, Herbert leaned on his horn.

OOOOOguh! OOOOOOOOOO guh!

Edgar hit the ground running and dragged Polly off the seat behind him. They were flying now, her feet hitting the ground at intervals. But Edgar was a city boy. He slowed, gasping and choking, and they were still too far away. He played a bit of crack the whip, catapulting Polly on ahead.

She ran. She ran harder. Her lungs screamed at her to slow down. She couldn't breathe.

No! God was here to help. He would! She ran.

Far off to the right stood a little knot of Aborigines, watching. Straight ahead were quiet groups of two or three. If she could just reach the city fathers . . . someone in command . . .

She could see the heartless scaffold clearly now. All attentions were turned to some point half a block beyond the scaffold. They were bringing him!

A portly gentleman stood just ahead. He was well-dressed, looking more a part of Sydney than some

189

mining camp. She called to him and her voice was louder than she expected it to be.

He turned to look at her. "Wait! No!" she tried to say. His eyes bulged wide. He recognized her.

"I'm Polly—Chase—" she gasped. "Come!"

She was going to grab his arm, but he jerked her to a halt. His eyes blazed anger, as if she were spoiling someone's fun. With a yank he started dragging her backward, in the wrong direction! Could it be that of all these onlookers, Polly had come upon Mr. Leadbetter?

Polly tried to struggle but her legs were too weak. Yet, she must—

"Whup!" The man grunted suddenly and let her go. He crumpled in the dirt, dragging her into the dust with him. She rolled free as a powerful hand gripped her elbow and whisked her bodily to her feet.

"David! Oh, David! Thank God!" How her heart sang to see that happy grin with the one tooth missing!

He wagged a digging stick, a waddy. "He weren't a goanna, but it works allasame." He took off at his long-legged, ground-eating lope, literally dragging her along. He seemed terribly good-natured for a man about to lose his best friend. "No worries!" he shot over his shoulder affably.

No worries?!

She saw Colm now for the first time. Flanked by armed men, he was climbing the scaffold steps in that blue shirt with the sleeves rolled up. They rose by measured degrees above the heads of the ghoulish spectators.

"Wait! Don't! I'm Polly Chase!" Her mind formed the words clearly and distinctly, but her faltering lips and lungs released them all a-shambles. Still some of the people here on the fringe heard her and turned.

A burly miner stared at her a moment and bellowed "Hold on there!" In a voice loud enough to frighten bulls, he thundered "Wait!" and snatched her other hand. He took off at a lope. Polly was barely touching the ground now, pulled along by these two strong and tireless men.

The miner roared the news again. Others in the crowd relayed the cry to the scaffold.

There was Louise near the foot of the gibbet! She was shaking her fist at Colm or something. This whole scene was surreal, the nightmare magnified by Polly's sheer exhaustion.

Oblivious, the hangman was adjusting the knot around Colm's neck. Finally someone near the scaffold was yelling to him. His hands already on the trapdoor rope, he turned to look toward Polly. Now everything would be all right!

"No!" Louise was shrieking. "No! You won't get him! Not you!" She howled at the hangman, "Do it! Do it!"

Everyone now was watching Polly. They knew! They knew!

Wailing, Louise leaped, cat-quick, up the scaffold steps. She snatched the trapdoor rope from the hangman's hands and yanked mightily.

Colm dropped through.

Polly screamed. She could not stop screaming. She could not even say his name because her voice kept screaming. After all this, it was too late! Louise had . . . had . . . had. . . .

No, God, please! Make it all untrue!

They arrived at the foot of the scaffold. They were here, now that it was all over, too late. Peter was gone. Colm was gone. Both losses so unjust, both so unworthy of death—

In a thunderous voice the miner was announcing to the world who she was—now that it was too late.

Polly collapsed against David as her screams trickled away into convulsive sobs. She was bathed in sweat; David was not even overly warm from the run. The two men she loved most in her life—

David must be grieving as much as she, but he sounded as though he were laughing. He shook her.

He gripped both her arms and pried her loose from his breast. "Hey! No worries!" He grinned as wide as Kansas.

Her mouth would not speak clearly. "But I love him, David! I love him!"

"Right-o," David chuckled. "So love 'im. Here he is." He turned her in a half circle around.

There he stood. His massive presence filled the whole world. And it was he; it was really truly he, as solid and stalwart as ever. Only an angry red rope burn along one side of his neck betrayed his ordeal.

Her knees were turning flaccid again, just as they always did when she needed them most. But she didn't really need them now. He was pulling her in against himself, encasing her in an overpowering bear hug, fusing her to him that their hearts could pound together as one.

She brought herself under control by degrees. It was over, and she must be strong.

It was over.

She gulped air a few minutes, then tried to hold her breath to stop the sobbing. It didn't work.

"We did it! We made it!" Herbert Towne's exuberant whoop pierced through all the other excited voices.

A man in a faded jacket gripped Polly's shoulder and turned her toward himself. Colm's arms loosened.

"Your full name?"

"Paulette Belinda Upshaw Chase. Polly."

"Describe your horse and wagon."

"Seventeen-year-old blue roan mare named Jewel with a sandcrack in the off front hoof. Flat-hound farm wagon with iron wheels. Convertible to shafts or tongue. But they're not mine anymore. I gave them to Colm here."

"You received checks. From what agency?"

"Department of the Army, Melbourne office. And some drafts from the local dry goods merchant, payment for lace."

"And your husband's full name?"

"Peter Murchison Chase; Murchison after his mother's side."

The man nodded. "All the right answers, and none of them she could've gotten from the papers. The *Murchison* was only from the parcel of books sent to Stawell. On bookplates, as was her maiden name *Upshaw.*"

A gaggle of what must be big-city reporters, all with notebooks and bowler hats, erupted into bedlam.

Above the ruction rang Herbert's voice loud and clear:

"All right, folks, who wants to travel to the nearest operating telegraph key? Make me an offer! Not you, Edgar. You go for free."

An angular lady with her hair pulled into a severe bun pushed in beside Polly, practically shouldering Colm aside. Bubbling excitedly, she read from her notebook. "Are you aware of Colm Stawell's last words? I write down last words, you know. He said, and I quote, 'When you find the woman I'm supposed to have killed, tell her I loved her to the end.' Did you hear him?"

Two other people interrupted with questions.

"Let her rest!" Colm barked gruffly in a tone of voice that quieted things momentarily, as if embarrassed somehow. He piloted her by the shoulders to a timbered lift of some sort a hundred feet off, a small poppethead.

"Colm? Louise—How could she do that—? What's—?"

He drew her in close, his back to the scaffold and the babbling tangle of people, sealing her away from the hubbub. "Found some things out about Louise. She didn't just leave Adelaide to start a new life for herself. She was labeled an undesirable in the district and forced out."

"Undesirable? Why?"

"It seemed she wanted some fellow's white horse and he chose not to give or sell it. Badgered him for weeks. When he threatened to get the constabulary

193

after her, she slipped into his stable one night and shot the horse dead. They couldn't actually prove she did it, but they were satisfied it was she—enough that they gave her a choice of leaving or undergoing a thorough background investigation and possibly mental treatment."

"Like the puppy. Maggie's puppy wasn't the first."

"Looks so. After you left, I seriously considered settling down, and Louise seemed a good girl to settle down with. She had her spells—I didn't know about the horse at the time—but I figured as she grew in the Lord, He could take care of any problem. She was more than willing. I was just about ready to get married.

"Then I happened to re-read First Corinthians. Paul says don't be unevenly yoked with an unbeliever. And she was, of course, an unbeliever. I showed her the gospel many a time, and I told her how I felt. Even before I thought of marrying her, even if it never happened, her soul was the important thing. But she didn't understand.

"And in Ephesians, chapter five, the man's called to love his wife and there was only one woman I loved. It wasn't Louise. I couldn't marry her and keep a clear conscience before God. My mistake was in telling her so."

"Flew into a rage."

He wagged his head. "That rage when she couldn't get the puppy was a pale imitation. She swore to get me for thinking I was too good for her. Went crooked on me like you wouldn't believe."

"But that's not how you felt! I know you better than that."

"She and some other other fellows got their heads together—men who'd like to dig my opals; men who think I'm too thick with the blacks; Louise, who was afraid you'd come back somehow and get me. They built a case, and—"

"I heard. Clever, in a way—in a twisted way." Polly laid her head against that reassuring expanse of blue chambray. "From the moment I heard about this on the train coming north, all I could think of was why God would let it happen. You're His servant. How could He let Louise and those blokes get away with it?"

His deep happy chuckle rippled through his chest and tickled her ear. "I felt a bit abandoned there at first, myself. Finally decided if Paul and Silas could sing in prison, so could I. Not sing—not this jackaroo. But *talk*. The ratbags the rest of the world gave up on, the drongos who drank too many of their opals away— they listened to the Word with pleasure. The turnkey let me have my Bible—Peter's Bible—and I could do good things for the Lord."

She giggled. "I didn't think you could just sit still and be idle."

"More'n that. More important, it opened my eyes to the need. It's something I want to do for the Lord on a regular basis, 'cause no one else is. Guess I had a hope even at the end there, that this mess would be put to rights. Even walking up the scaffold steps, I was still hoping."

She lifted her head away. All this swirled on the surface of her mind. It would take days to sink in. "But Louise pulled the rope! I saw you drop. The burn on your neck there—" She touched the sticky raw mark gently, gingerly, with a fingertip to confirm it somehow.

"That I can't explain." Colm looked off beyond her shoulder. "But maybe you can."

Polly turned. Loose and easy, David was leaning against a timber, grinning.

"Maybe." David's shirt was off now, and the cicatrices traced across his chest told the world about his manhood. Yet he sounded like a cheerful little child. "Y'know them two jackaroos by the barber shop couple weeks ago, Mate? Said loud where we could hear 'em—said they couldn't stand black skin. Trying to pick a fight."

"I remember. What about them?"

"Last night before the moon, there they stand by the scaffold—me-to-you away from the scaffold, eh? Them very two. I took off all my whitefeller clothes." David snapped his fingers. "Can't see David no more; same color night. Climbed up the scaffold, up top. Them standing right there, too. Never see me, don't hear me. I cut the rope almost through, 'way up you can't see the cut." All those teeth less one gleamed brightly. "No worries."

"No worries," Colm echoed. "No, David, there is one worry left." He tipped Polly's face back to his, meeting her eye to eye. "What about Peter? You didn't abandon Peter, did you?"

At last, after all the turmoil and weary miles and panic, her own smile could loosen up and break through. Polly felt suddenly jubilant. Her poor heart, which had been so sorely used this last day or two, filled up with joy at long, long last. Her relief and happiness welled up and poured out and would no longer fit inside her.

Over at the scaffold beyond Colm's shoulder, Louise sat on the platform edge with her feet dangling, her face buried in her hands. Herbert had managed to get his big White truck into the thick of the crowd now. The bonnet was raised on it and four or five people were up to their elbows in his engine. The fellow in the faded jacket, apparently a constable of some sort, was holding that crowd of city reporters at bay, with the miner at his side, but they wouldn't be able to hold that mob back forever. Polly and Colm would have to face them soon. Polly was even now, at the very back of her mind, planning which raw facts they would give the world at large, and what part of the story ought to be reserved exclusively for Edgar Seavers. He had helped so enthusiastically, and apparently his career could use the boost.

Good. All right. Everything was all right. No worries. She laughed out loud at David's one-size-fits-all appraisal for every situation. She fingered the opal at her throat. She smiled, her heart singing, into Colm's deep gray eyes.

"When I got that letter—remember? You said the army doesn't believe in fairy tales. But it's a fairy-tale ending, after all."

MEET THE AUTHOR ·

Sandy Dengler

SANDY DENGLER was born and raised in Ohio, earning her bachelor's degree at Bowling Green State University, but early on developed wanderlust. She obtained the master's degree in zoology/desert ecology at Arizona State and married a National Park Service ranger. That helped the wanderlust; they have lived since then in national parks from coast to coast, raising two daughters here and there.

Soon after Sandy and the elder daughter shared dreams of someday seeing Australia, the daughter came home with reservations on Qantas. It was a glorious trip!* And the best part of it? The mother/daughter travelers returned home as friend/friend.

*Highly recommended; wonderful country, Australia, though persons accustomed to the speech of, for instance, New Jersey, might have trouble with verbal communication. Australia's written language, however, is similar to ours.